Hot Latin Docs

Sultry, sexy bachelor brothers on the loose!

Santiago, Alejandro, Rafael
and Dante Valentino are Miami's most eligible
doctors. Yet the brothers' dazzling lives
hide a darker truth—one which made these
determined bachelors close their hearts
to love years ago…

But now four feisty women are about to
turn the heat up for these sexy Latin docs and
tempt them each to do something they never
imagined…get down on one knee!

Find out what happens in:

Santiago's Convenient Fiancée
by Annie O'Neil

Alejandro's Sexy Secret
by Amy Ruttan

Rafael's One Night Bombshell
by Tina Beckett

Dante's Shock Proposal
by Amalie Berlin

All available now!

Dear Reader,

Sometimes the past comes back to haunt us in a thousand different ways: the painful decisions we've made, the difficulties we've faced…those hard goodbyes we were never quite ready to say. This is exactly the situation epidemiologist Rafael Valentino finds himself in. Until he crosses paths one night with a beautiful neonatologist who challenges every belief he holds. Maybe it's because Cassie Larrobee has faced her own set of hardships—a set of circumstances which threatens to stand in the way of enduring happiness.

I dearly loved these two characters. They made me laugh and cry…and hope.

Thank you for joining Rafe and Cassie as they struggle to overcome emotional barriers that have been many years in the making. And maybe—just maybe—this special couple will find love along the way.

I hope you enjoy their journey as much as I loved writing about it. Happy reading!

Love,

Tina Beckett

RAFAEL'S
ONE NIGHT
BOMBSHELL

BY
TINA BECKETT

Published in Great Britain 2017
By Mills & Boon, an imprint of HarperCollins*Publishers*
1 London Bridge Street, London, SE1 9GF

© 2017 Tina Beckett

ISBN: 978-0-263-06837-5

Our policy is to use papers that are natural, renewable and recyclable
products and made from wood grown in sustainable forests. The logging
and manufacturing processes conform to the legal environmental
regulations of the country of origin.

Printed and bound in Great Britain
by CPI Antony Rowe, Chippenham, Wiltshire

Three-times Golden Heart® finalist **Tina Beckett** learned to pack her suitcases almost before she learned to read. Born to a military family, she has lived in the United States, Puerto Rico, Portugal and Brazil. In addition to travelling, Tina loves to cuddle with her pug, Alex, spend time with her family, and hit the trails on her horse. Learn more about Tina from her website, or 'friend' her on Facebook.

Books by Tina Beckett

Mills & Boon Medical Romance

Christmas Miracles in Maternity

The Nurse's Christmas Gift

The Hollywood Hills Clinic

Winning Back His Doctor Bride

Her Playboy's Secret
Hot Doc from Her Past
Playboy Doc's Mistletoe Kiss
A Daddy for Her Daughter

Visit the Author Profile page
at millsandboon.co.uk for more titles.

To my family. As always. I love you!

PROLOGUE

THE STRANGER AT the bar was as miserable as she was.

At least, judging from the three empty shot glasses in front of him, he was. He rolled a fourth glass between his thumb and index finger, staring at the amber contents as if looking for something he'd lost.

Kind of like she was. Only she hadn't exactly lost anything. It was more like it had been thrown away. Echoes of her childhood.

You can do this.

Taking a deep breath, Cassandra Larrobee unscrewed the huge rock from the ring finger of her left hand and dropped it into her purse. It was better than drowning it in the storm drain just outside the door but not nearly as satisfying. She should have realized long ago that permanent relationships weren't in the cards for her.

She scrubbed at the indentation left by the ring, hesitating for the barest second, and then walked across the floor of Mad Ron's, heading for the only available barstool—the one right next to the stranger.

Little Heliconia's go-to bar, Mad Ron's was named after its eccentric owner and had been one of Miami's most revered liquor joints for many years. It also happened to be the first one she'd come across during her flight from the scene of the crime.

Her fiancé's crime.

The loud clink of glasses and raucous laughter provided a much-needed refuge. A sanctuary. And if the man at the bar was willing to raise a glass with her, all the better. It would be a brief visit—not long enough to become attached. "Temporary" was a state of being that Cassie knew how to rock. And she could at least blur the memory of what she'd seen tonight, even if she couldn't blot it out entirely.

After that, she needed to find a new place to live.

She slung her purse over her shoulder as she reached her destination and parked her butt on the tall stool. Ron himself appeared in front of her, puffs of white hair and a pink Hawaiian print shirt making her smile.

Before he could even open his mouth to ask, she said, "I'll have what he's having."

Where had that come from?

"Sure thing, *chica.*" As Ron reached behind the bar for a bottle, the stranger's head swiveled toward her, his fingers still twirling the tiny glass. And those eyes… Straddling the line between brown and predatory, they caught at her, snatching away whatever clever quip she'd been getting ready to toss his way.

Clever? That was so not a word Cassie would use to describe herself.

Capable? Careful? Cautious?

Yep. Cs—all three of them. Only right now she was none of those things.

"Do you even know what I'm having?" He held his little glass up, the low lighting in the bar making the amber contents seem darker. More dangerous.

Or maybe that was the man himself.

"I'm sure I can handle whatever it is."

The bartender set a matching shot glass in front of her. Suddenly she wasn't quite sure she *could* handle it. But it was either slink off or gut it out. And Cassie was no quitter. Except when given no other choice.

She lifted her glass and clinked it against his, before putting it to her lips and chugging the contents down in one swallow.

There. As easy as taking medici—

Liquid fire consumed her throat, her abdomen suddenly spasming as the fumes sought escape. She forced her eyes to remain on his as he downed his own drink, somehow managing to suppress the cough building in her chest. Letting out a quick gust of air that she hoped would ease the pain, she thunked her glass down on the bar. Just like in the movies.

"Another?" Ron held up a half-empty bottle.

One corner of the stranger's mouth curved as he continued to watch her, setting his own glass down with a mere whisper of sound. He knew, damn him. Knew that she was a lightweight as far as the drinking game went. Not that she would even try to outdo him. His last drink upped his total to four. She would be passed out on the polished surface of the bar before she got to three.

So she changed tack. "I'll have a margarita this time around."

Mad Ron was known around Miami for making the best in the area. And it was a drink she could sip— slowly—rather than slug.

"Rafe? What'll you have?"

"I'll have coffee. Black."

What?

"Coming right up."

Damn. She couldn't even get a stranger to drink with her on this sorry-ass evening. But she did know the stranger's name now. Not that it mattered.

She swiveled her barstool a little to the right to face him. "Too much for you?"

"I'll let you know a little bit later."

The air caught in her lungs.

Was he talking about the drinks? Her own head felt a little woozy, but she was pretty sure it had nothing to do with what she'd just drunk and everything to do with the man sitting beside her.

Well, why the hell not? Her fiancé had played the cheating game, why shouldn't she?

Was it still considered cheating if the engagement was over?

It didn't matter. She could consider this the denoue-ment of that failed relationship.

Ron slid a glass toward her. The huge bowl was precariously perched on top of a glass stem, the lime expertly stabbed onto the salted rim.

Oh, my. She'd forgotten how ginormous these things were. Ron must have seen her indecision because he set Rafe's coffee in front of him and cocked a brow at her. "Everything okay?"

"I think I've changed my mind. Could I have a cof-fee as well?"

"Sure thing, *chica.*" Ron gave her a wink, picked up her glass and called out to his customers. "Anyone want a margarita? On the house."

Within seconds her drink had found a new home, and she had a steaming *café con leche* in its place.

"Thanks." Maybe the splash of milk would help cool the whiskey that was still sending flames darting through her stomach. Or was that warm licking sensation caused by something else entirely?

"So," the stranger said, taking a drink of his coffee, "thanks to Ron, you know my name, but I don't know yours."

And she didn't want him to. Her thoughts whipped through a couple of sharp responses, rejecting each one. She was never going to see him again, so what did it matter what name she gave him?

"Bonnie." She crossed her fingers beneath the bar, hoping her dearest friend would forgive her for pulling her name out of the hat.

Rafe took another sip, regarding her with inscrutable eyes. "You don't look like a Bonnie."

"No?" She swallowed hard. "What do I look like?"

"Like a beautiful woman who just got out of a painful relationship."

Shock wheeled through her system. "Excuse me?"

How could he have known that? Or was it just some kind of pickup line?

His fingers moved to her left hand, which was lying flat on the bar, and slid up her ring finger, rubbing across the base of it. "The ring just came off. I saw you drop it in your purse right before you came over here. Unless you're just looking for a good time. And you don't seem like that kind of girl."

This time she wasn't going to lie. "I'm not. So what are you in here for?" She motioned toward the empty glasses. "Or do you simply get hammered every night?"

"Oh." His thumb rubbed across her finger again,

sending more heat shooting through her veins. "I am not hammered. Not by a long shot."

The bartender knew his name, though, so he was a regular. She came in with friends from time to time, but not often enough for Ron to actually know her by name. Thank goodness. Otherwise he might just tell this man what it was. And she didn't want that.

"Four whiskeys is a lot to drink at one time."

"Maybe. But I've celebrated this day at Ron's for the last eighteen years or so. I think I know my limit."

Okay, she had no idea how to respond to that, since his voice hinted that the date didn't hold good memories. Especially not if he spent the night getting drunk every year.

Death of a spouse? A child? Divorce?

Each option went through her head, but there was no way she could voice any of them aloud. The doctor in her came to the surface, however, and she couldn't help but ask. "You don't normally drive yourself home, do you?"

"No. I spend the night at a hotel just around the corner."

She blinked. There was something about the way he said those words…

Oh.

"You're not alone when you go there."

"No."

She glanced at the coffee mug in front of him. Why had he suddenly stopped drinking?

Maybe for the same reason she'd found her way to this particular barstool and engaged a handsome man in conversation. Was it just to get back at her ex?

Yes. And why not? Darrin would never know. But

she would. And she could show the universe that she too knew how to play the game.

She lifted her chin. "I wasn't planning on leaving here alone either."

His thumb paused its stroking for just a second. "Did you have your sights on anyone in particular?"

"I'm talking to him."

Cassie couldn't believe she'd just said that. But why the hell shouldn't she have a little bit of fun? If he was celebrating something dark and disturbing, then that made two of them.

Unless he was a serial killer or something. Maybe she should check just to make sure. She blurted out, "So, how do you know Ron?"

"My family has known him for years. Including *mi hermanos*."

He'd lapsed into Spanish with such ease that he must speak it regularly. He didn't mention his mother or father, however. Just his brothers. Regardless, it was doubtful he was a Jack the Ripper type if his family and Ron's were friends. Ron was a great judge of character, from what she'd seen and heard.

Speaking of the devil, the bartender appeared back in front of them. "How are things?"

"I think we're about ready to get out of here." Rafe pulled out his wallet and dropped some serious-looking cash on the counter.

"I can pay for my own drink," she said to cover the disappointment caused by the loss of his touch.

"You can get them the next time."

There wouldn't be a next time, and they both knew it. But it was either sit there and argue, and possibly ruin the delicious awareness that had been slowly building in her, or let it go.

She let it go. This lie was one she could overlook. Unlike her fiancé's declarations that "It wasn't what it looked like." Things were normally exactly how they seemed. No longer want a child? Transfer them to another home. Tired of your fiancée? Move on to the next woman.

Want a temporary fling? Head to Mad Ron's Bar.

Yep, she definitely knew how to play.

"Next time," she murmured.

He stood, shoving his wallet into the back pocket of his black jeans.

For a second she thought he was planning on leaving. Alone. Until he held out his hand.

There was still time to chicken out. To sit there like she didn't have a clue what he meant. Except she'd basically told him she wanted to hook up with him.

So she slid her fingers into his, relishing the way they enfolded hers in a strong grip. Her stomach somersaulted as she allowed her legs to swing to the floor. They shook, but somehow she braced her high-heeled sandals beneath her and remained standing. He said he normally went to a hotel a short distance away, but in little Heliconia there were several places that would fit that description. Some more respectable than others.

Who needed respectable for what they were about to do?

Not her, that was for sure.

Rafe towed her through the crowd and out the door. Twin pots of gardenias flanked the entrance, the breeze lifting the heavy fragrance of the blooms and sending it out into the night. She could hardly believe she was leaving a bar with a total stranger.

How long had it been since she'd done something so…dangerous?

And there was no mistaking that the man gripping her hand was dangerous, no matter how well he knew Ron. He was far removed from the world of her financier ex, who was busy building his empire— and amassing women as easily as he did money, evidently. Well, he was now down one percentage point. Or maybe since she'd been his fiancée, she was worth a little bit more, maybe a point and a half.

What had she learned through this experience? A stable career didn't always translate into a stable life.

Ha! Who needed stable when there were men like Rafe in the world?

They were halfway down the block before the man in question stopped to face her. His hands slid up her arms as he gazed into her face. "Are you sure about this?"

No, but she was not about to admit that. Hadn't she just said it had been ages since she'd let herself be picked up by a man in a bar? Actually, she'd never done that before. Well, she could now cross "Pick up stranger" off her bucket list.

Not that it had even been on there in the first place.

She took a deep breath and then nodded. "Yes. I'm sure. Unless you've changed your mind."

"About your name not being Bonnie? Or about this?"

Then his lips found hers and every other thought she'd had vanished.

The second they hit the room at the hotel, his fingers smoothed across her hair, quickly finding the elastic at the back of her head and sliding it over her locks, freeing the messy knot she'd formed before she'd gone out. The whole mass tumbled free, spilling halfway down her back.

Before she could even cringe over how crazy her waves probably were from the humidity of the day, his voice rumbled above her.

"Hermosa. Me encanta su cabello." Even as he murmured it, he wound her hair around his hand, tipping her head back. *"Tu novio es un idiota."*

The flood of Spanish whisked up her spine, her brain scooping up the words and translating them with ease.

Wow. The man was as hot as they came.

The fact that he'd called her fiancé an idiot made him even hotter. It also gave her a shot of courage. Winding her arms around his neck, she went up on tiptoe, surprised at how far she had to stretch to get to his lips. Too far. She couldn't reach, unless he bent down. "No more talking."

"Agreed."

His fingers went to the back of her fitted blouse and found the zipper, sliding it down with ease.

Okay. That was more like it. Sweet heat fizzed through her tummy and bubbled up her chest, making her shudder.

He stopped. "Okay?"

Far too okay. "Hurry."

Up went that sexy smile.

The zipper finished its journey, and the back of her blouse parted. His palm skimmed down her skin, seeking something but not finding it.

"Dios mío."

This time it was Cassie who smiled. She was small

enough that she didn't always wear a bra, and from his reaction she was glad today was one of those days. Coming here with him was the right thing to do. She was sure of it.

Her top fluttered over her shoulders and down her arms, landing on the floor at her feet. Rafe's fingertips trailed over her collarbone, but didn't venture any lower. Instead, he moved behind her, twisting her hair and dropping it over her left shoulder. It whispered over her nipple, sending a ripple of sensation through it that jetted straight to the region due south of her breasts. His lips went to the side of her neck, kissing softly, his teeth grazing the sensitive skin he found there.

"Bonnie, open your eyes."

The name jarred her, threatening to send her libido plummeting through the floor. Then she did as he asked, not even realizing she'd closed her eyes. She wasn't sure how he knew they were closed since he was behind her, and she couldn't see…

Her gaze found his.

That's how. There was a mirror over the dresser in front of her. She swallowed as she took in the two of them standing there. Rafe's head was still tilted, his lips less than an inch away from the skin he'd been kissing. All thoughts of the fake name skittered out of reach as his hands slowly skimmed up her abdomen, over her ribcage, his left palm dipping under her length of hair. When he reached her breasts he covered them. The sight was heady. And unsettling. And when his fingers parted, catching her nipples between them and pinching, her lids slammed shut again as a wave of need crashed over her.

He could take her right now, and she'd come.

That's what she wanted.

"Open."

She blinked again, although her eyes didn't seem to want to co-operate.

His teeth caught her neck, mimicking what his fingers were doing to her breasts. Squeeze. Release. Squeeze. Release.

"Open." His words were softer this time. Almost a growl.

Her eyes were already open, so what did he...

A knee nudged the back of hers.

Oh, lordy. Her lips parted, her lungs dragging in air that suddenly seemed still and heavy, while the spot between her legs pulsed with heat.

Somehow she made her feet shuffle apart, the heels of her shoes giving a warning wobble.

"Encantadora." His hips nudged forward, a ridge of hard flesh finding the groove between her buttocks. His hands left her breasts and traveled down to her hips, holding her in place while he slowly pressed against her again and again. All the while his gaze held hers in the mirror.

She was going to explode, very, very soon, if he didn't...

He stopped moving, and all her fears about things ending too soon screamed at her for being an idiot. His hands found hers and lifted them, placing them flat on the smooth wood of the dresser. *"Mantenerlos allí."*

Keep them right there.

Gulping, she somehow managed a nod, then felt an air-conditioned breeze slide over her calves, up the backs of her knees...her thighs.

Having her hands on the dresser had tipped her forward at the waist, and Rafe was gathering the fabric of her maxi-skirt in his hands, bunching it time and time again, until the whole length of it was up over her behind, baring her legs and exposing her underwear. Not a thong, but small enough that she started to shift.

"Don't move."

Heaving in breath after breath, she watched as he removed his wallet, opening it and removing a small packet. Here it came. The moment of truth. If she was going to tell him no, now was the time to do it.

Are you kidding me?

Her body evidently had a mind of its own, because it was screaming all sorts of protests at her.

He set the packet on top of one of her hands, sending another shiver through her. Did he want her to take it?

No. He'd told her to leave her hands where they were.

She heard the snick of another zipper. His, this time.

Cassie's breath locked in her lungs when the elastic of her panties tightened and then slid over the curve of her backside until they rested just below it, one palm curving around the front of her thigh until he reached the heart of her.

Her body seized as a finger slid into her with ease.

"Ahhhh." She was powerless to hold back the sound.

"Caliente. Mojado. Tal como esperaba."

The rational side of her should feel embarrassed that with barely any effort at all he'd aroused her to fever pitch. And he knew it. But the not-so-rational side felt a stab of pride that her body had obeyed him.

All too soon, his hand withdrew. When she started to mutter a protest, he stopped her.

"Shhhh. Almost."

He retrieved the condom from its resting place and ripped it open in front of her. He lifted it and stroked it down her cheek and over her lips. It was unbearably sexy. She could picture him against her mouth, asking to come in.

She wanted it. Wanted to feel him along her tongue.

"Tell me you want me."

"I do." Her eyes closed and then opened again, fixing on his. "I want you."

"Yes."

The condom disappeared below her line of vision, but she could picture him slowly rolling the latex cover over his length. His mouth went to her cheek, following the line he'd taken seconds before. She turned her head so she could kiss him. Their lips fused together as Rafe's hands returned to her hips, easing them backward, tilting them, his mouth following hers as his movements forced her upper body toward the top of the dresser, until her breasts were resting on the wooden surface.

"Open. More."

He definitely wasn't talking about her mouth. She spread her legs wide, his chest pushing against her back, hands returning to her breasts.

With a quick thrust of his hips, he entered her, stretching her wider than she thought possible. He stayed like that, their labored breathing the only sound in the room for several long seconds. Then his thumbs were brushing across her nipples, and it was as if he was caressing her somewhere else. A sharp point of arousal began building rapidly, threatening to overtake her.

"Rafe...I don't think I can... Please."

"Say my name. Again."

"Rafe."

Then he was moving with powerful strokes, sending her hips into the edge of the dresser, the sharp pain only adding to the pleasure.

It was too much. The wave found her. Slammed into her and sent her spinning through the surf, taking her breath away and making her see stars.

She was vaguely aware of Rafe above her, shouting something in Spanish, but she was too lost to try to make sense of it as he thrust into her again and again.

Then it was over. His cheek against hers, nostrils flaring as he dragged in air.

Her own body eased its grip on her senses, and she blinked. The mirror showed that his eyes were closed. She swallowed.

Who would he be when those dark pupils met hers again?

She shifted, trying to brace herself for an abrupt withdrawal. A speedy exit into the night.

"Don't move." The eyes opened.

"But…"

His body slid from hers, but it was anything but abrupt. He turned her to face him. "Do you have to leave yet?"

The words sounded as if they'd been forced from him against his will. His sudden frown echoed that thought.

She should. She should go, tossing him a quick thank you on her way out the door. But she didn't want to. To leave was to face the ugly reality that awaited her outside that door. "No. I don't have to leave."

One side of his mouth curved, his frown fading as

he swung her into his arms. "Then let's see if we can try that again. In the comfort of a bed this time."

He leaned down and nipped her lower lip. "As great and sexy as that was, it was much faster than I'd hoped it would be. So for the next round…"

He tipped her shoulders down so he could catch at the edge of the bedspread and pull it down. "Let's see just how slow we can go." With that he set her down on the bed, went over to the dresser and retrieved his wallet. When he pulled out three more condoms, her eyes widened, and she had to moisten her lips.

Surely not.

As if reading her thoughts, he grinned again. "Oh, yes. We can. And we will."

Bonnie—if that was even her name—was sprawled naked on her stomach, her hair in a deliciously tangled mess all around her face. A peculiar twinge went through Rafe's gut as he stared down at her.

Shafts of sunlight were already ducking beneath the hem of the curtains and pooling on the carpet at the bottom of the bed. He was normally long gone by now, his one night binge doing what it always did: blotting out a specific memory.

Almost against his will, he took a step closer, noting her head was precariously perched near the edge of the mattress. The reason for that made a certain part of his body react yet again.

He should wake her up, make sure she got home safely, but something stopped him from touching her. He was due at work in a half hour, but it wasn't that.

He'd approached last night the same way as he did every year on this date, and yet something about this woman's appearance in the bar had been different. The way she'd jerked the ring off her finger as if she couldn't stand it being there one second longer. She'd looked lost, the sense of desperation in her eyes dragging up a sense of protectiveness he hadn't felt in a long time. Hadn't *wanted* to feel in a long time.

Rafe had thought for a moment she was running away from someone. He'd actually glanced behind her to make sure some abusive ex wasn't following her. When he'd satisfied himself that she was alone, he decided to bide his time and leave her to someone else.

Except she'd sat down beside him, the clear blue of her eyes colliding with his glance and sending all rational thought running for the door. Maybe the alcohol had actually done the job he'd meant it to do and addled his thinking. The rest was history.

So what did he do now that he was no longer under the influence?

She was a big girl. Surely she could hail a cab and get home on her own?

The notepad on the end table caught his attention, along with a black elastic circle.

When she'd reached for the band to put her hair up before settling down to sleep last night, he'd stopped her, the thick mass of strands calling for him to sift through them one more time…to wrap them around himself and…

Hell, she'd driven him wild last night. He closed his eyes to banish the memory.

Time to go. Now. Before he woke her up and made himself later for work than he was already going to be.

Besides, goodbyes were one thing he'd never learned to do well.

Going to the table, he gripped the pen, his fingers accidentally brushing across the hair band in the process. Without thinking, he picked it up and pocketed it, picturing her leaving the hotel with her locks in sexy disarray from what they'd done in this room.

He would probably be damned to eternity for everything that had happened last night.

No. The damning had taken place many years ago, when shaking eighteen-year-old hands had placed his signature at the bottom of an irrevocable document.

He grabbed the hotel stationery. This time there would be no signature. The pen hovered over the pristine white paper for several seconds as he thought. Then he scrawled two words. No *Goodbye*. No *Thanks for a fun evening*. Just: *Taxi fare*. Then opening his wallet one last time, he drew out a crisp fifty-dollar bill. Because unless he wanted to go snooping through her purse or, worse, wake her up to ask if she had any money, it was the only thing he could think of to do.

Laying the bill under the note, he set a cheesy palm tree alarm clock on top of it.

Then he quietly exited the room. This was one event that would go down in annals of What Not to Do with a Beautiful Woman.

Because every moan and touch and thrust was permanently seared in his skull. A cautionary tale at best. So the only thing left to do was tiptoe back to his normal mundane life and never think of Bonnie—or whatever her name was—ever again.

CHAPTER ONE

One month later...

EVEN AS CASSIE wrapped the measuring tape around Renato Silva's head, she knew. The newborn would fall below the circumference norms.

Microcephaly wasn't something she encountered every day. Or even every year. And yet this child made three in the last eight weeks. A shiver went up her spine. With all of the reports coming out of Brazil and elsewhere, she worried that these cases could somehow be related.

Two centimeters below normal. Not terribly off, but still concerning.

One of the nurses glanced at her, brows up. Cassie knew what she was asking. She gave a subtle nod in response, her stomach churning inside her. And it was up to her to give the new mom the news. The obstetrician had already moved on to the next laboring patient.

She cradled the baby in her arms, and switched to Portuguese. *"Você fala inglês?"*

"Yes. Some. I am learning." The young woman's hungry eyes took in the swaddled infant. Her child. A tiny soul carrying a wealth of hopes and dreams.

Two centimeters surely wouldn't destroy all of those dreams. She'd seen babies with terrible deficits go further than anyone had ever thought possible.

The baby gave a hoarse cry. It was a touch more strident than that of most newborns. Another worrying sign.

"Renato is breathing just fine and his color is good. We'll want to run a few tests—"

"Something is wrong." With those soft, knowing words, the whole atmosphere in the room changed.

Cassie couldn't keep it from her, not and live with herself. "His head is a little bit smaller than we'd like to see, but we won't know anything for sure until we check him out completely."

Her patient fell back onto the pillows. "It was the sickness. I left…came here in December to get away from it. *Ele me seguiu.*"

It followed me.

The words sent a chill through her. "What sickness? You were sick while you were pregnant?"

"Yes. Just after I learned I carried him. I fear it was Zika."

News and panic about the mosquito-borne virus had been a huge topic among doctors and journalists for the last year. Yes, she knew of it. This was the third incidence of microcephaly at the hospital. Like it or not, it was time to call the CDC again. She knew they were swamped—it was the excuse they'd given her three weeks ago when the second microcephaly case had appeared. They'd told her they'd get to her as soon as possible. But this time they had to listen to her. Her patients' lives depended on it.

"You know for certain you had Zika?"

"I was sick. The mosquitoes, they were very bad."

It was just turning summertime in the U.S. but since the seasons were the opposite on the southern side of the globe, December was the hottest part of the year in Brazil.

Her stomach took another turn, whether from the tragedy unfolding in front of her or from something else, she had no idea. She swallowed hard, trying to rid herself of the queasy feeling. It stayed with her no matter how much she tried to banish it.

"I'll come back and talk to you as soon as we check Renato over." She squeezed the woman's shoulder. "I promise."

Cassie nodded at the nurse to take the baby to the nursery, where they would carefully go over the newborn inch by inch.

But first...

She walked through the door and pulled her cell phone from the pocket of her lab coat. First, she was going to call the CDC in Washington one more time and give whoever answered a piece of her mind.

The canopy of the paraglider caught the wind and swept Rafael Valentino's legs out from under him as it lifted him skyward. Still attached to the towline behind the boat, the wind whistled past his face, plastering his hair to his head. A familiar sense of weightlessness took over, allowing his problems to drop to the warm sands of the beach below, where they would stay until he touched down. A few more seconds, and he could relax into his harness. But not yet.

Rafe had flown more in the past month than he had in years. Not since those early terrible days after his father's death, when the adrenaline rush had been one of the few things that had allowed him to blot out the reality of what had happened.

At a signal from the speedboat driver, he pulled the cord that would release the towline and set him free to glide for as long as the winds would sustain his flight. He sat, his harness cradling his butt and his thighs as he worked on changing his angle, catching the winds much as a sailboat did. Only there was something about being in the air, suspended far above the earth. It was heaven. There was nothing else like it.

Except for maybe those last frantic seconds of being suspended in a different kind of heaven. Like the one a month ago?

His jaw tightened. Thoughts like that were why he was out here today. He had to work in a few hours, but he'd needed something to erase those memories. Bonnie had been different in some indefinable way.

And the last thing he wanted to do was try to define anything about that night.

A sudden gust of air caused the nylon that covered the baffle cells to flutter, and he bobbed a time or two before his flight settled back out. The change in the wind conditions did the trick. Everything was wiped from his brain except for controlling his craft.

It was a perfect day for flying, and there were dots of color all up and down the beach as others had the same idea. Powerboats far below carved out white wakes in the ocean as some of the commercial parasail ventures towed thrill seekers up and down the coastline. He would have to descend with care when the time came, but he already had his landing site mapped out.

For now, he would just immerse himself in the moment and not let anything else clutter his skull. He adjusted the speed bar at his feet and shifted his weight to change direction.

Nothing could bother him here.

A sudden buzzing at his hip stopped that thought in its tracks. Damn.

Really? His phone? He should have turned it off. Glancing down and trying to read the caller ID while it was upside down, he swore softly when he was able to make it out.

Perfect. It was work. His boss wouldn't call him on his day off unless it was urgent.

Fun time was over almost before it began. Scouring the beach for a place to land that was relatively free of sun worshippers, he shifted his weight once again and began his descent.

An hour later, Rafe was striding down the hallway of Seaside Hospital. He'd been hopping from facility to facility in the last several weeks, trying to keep up with the number of worried doctors and patients who were raising the alarm. It was the same in a lot of other cities—especially those in the South. The warmer the temperatures, the more likely a rogue virus was to dig in and spread. His home country of Heliconia was under a red alert, pregnant travelers being warned to stay away, just as they were in Brazil and most parts of Central and South America.

Zika had been around for decades, but for some reason it was now spreading quickly, crossing continents and the placental barrier alike, and wreaking havoc wherever it went. And the growing stack of evidence said that the virus could infiltrate host cells and cause insidious health problems for whoever was infected, long after the illness itself was gone.

Zika was the new Lyme disease.

Worse, new studies were showing it could be sexually transmitted from a man to his partner.

The hope was that a vaccine would be developed quickly, but until then, all Rafe could do was put out fires. Like the one he'd tried to drown a month ago at Mad Ron's. He'd ended up having to put out a completely different fire that night.

His hand went to his pocket, fingers fiddling with the circle of elastic he'd been carrying around ever since then. He had no idea why he'd picked it up off the dresser, or why he hadn't thrown it away in the weeks that followed.

A trophy?

No. He'd never brought anything home from his other encounters. But Bonnie had been different somehow. There'd been a frenzied desperation to her lovemaking that had matched his own.

Killing old demons?

It didn't matter. He removed his hand from his pocket and forced his mind back to his obligations. He was here to meet the head neonatologist at the hospital, along with the head maternity nurse and the hospital administrator. He called up a file on his phone to retrieve their names. He only recognized one of them.

Bonnie Maxwell.

That's why he'd shoved the tie in his pocket, although it was doubtful it was the same woman. And he'd never learned what her last name was.

And if she was the same Bonnie from the bar? Was

he going to hand over the elastic and say, "Here you go. Sorry it went missing."

He snorted, turning a corner and following the signs on the wall. Not hardly. He was not going to admit to picking it up from the dresser, although the thread of guilt for abandoning her the morning after their encounter was still there as strong as ever. A peculiar longing had fermented in his stomach and sent a sour broth splashing up his throat as he'd stared down at her. He'd taken things too far by not getting drunk enough before taking her back to the hotel. He'd started drinking coffee far too soon.

Cynthia Porter, Administrator. This was the place. He knocked, feet braced wide in preparation for what he might find inside.

"Come in."

Rafe pushed through the door to find three women seated in the office.

The sight of sun-kissed locks tied into a familiar scrunchy mass made his stomach contract all over again, although she was facing away from him.

It was the same woman. It had to be.

Damn. Mistake number two: not making sure his date for the night was in a profession other than medicine.

The woman behind the desk stood. "Dr. Valentino?"

"Yes, and you must be Ms. Porter."

He watched the blonde, who still hadn't turned her head. There was no indication that his last name was familiar. Maybe because they'd never exchanged surnames. Or maybe she was much cooler than she'd seemed four weeks ago. Was the ring still off?

The third woman had already looked over at him

with a smile, the tossing of red curls giving her a mischievous air.

"Thank you for coming, although it was Dr. Larrobee who discovered the connection between some of our newborns. Let me introduce you."

Both women stood. And when Bonnie finally turned around to face him she gasped, every bit of color leaching from her face.

The administrator either ignored the sound or hadn't heard it, because she continued with the introductions. "This is Bonnie Maxwell and Dr. Cassandra Larrobee. Cassie is the one who notified your office about the cases."

His gaze remained glued to the blonde's, his hand diving back into his pocket and finding the hair tie. "Bonnie and I have already made each other's acquaintance."

Blue eyes went wide, and she gave a barely perceptible shake of her head.

What the hell?

"I'm sorry? Have we met?" The words didn't come from her but from the redhead, and his attention shifted to her.

Ah, so that was it.

One side of Rafe's mouth twitched. He should have known. He *had* known actually, although he couldn't prove it until now. His glance tracked back, and he couldn't resist a murmured, "Liar, liar…"

Pants on fire.

Only her pants hadn't been the only thing on fire that night. Her touch had scorched like wildfire across his senses.

Crimson washed into her face, gray stormy flecks

appearing in those expressive eyes. "I think he got the names mixed up, but Ra...er, Dr. Valentino and I have met on one occasion."

The redhead gave her a quick nudge with her shoulder. "Cassie, wow. You didn't tell me!"

The administrator frowned. "You've already met to discuss the cases?"

Cassandra... Cassie—now *that* name fit her.

"No, I...we..." Her voice trailed away.

"We have a mutual acquaintance here in town." He might not be able to count good old Jack D. since Cassie had obviously never shaken hands with a glass of whiskey in her life. But Mad Ron had definitely recognized her. And since he and Ron went way back, it wasn't a lie. At least, not the whopper of a lie that "Bonnie" had been.

Cassie's shoulders slumped, probably in relief. "Yes, we do."

The woman who had to be Bonnie muttered something that sounded like, "Girlfriend, you and I need to have a long discussion."

So that's why she'd used the name. These two were friends. His smile widened. "Now that the introductions are out of the way, why don't we sit down and discuss the cases, and you can share your concerns. In return, I'll tell you what I know."

Well, maybe not *everything* he knew, like that cute little dimple she had on her left shoulder blade. Or the way her soft murmurs had caused a chain reaction in him that wouldn't be denied.

"I've got the files ready in the meeting room down the hall," said Ms. Porter. "Shall we? There's coffee in there as well."

He would need bucketfuls of caffeine to knock him back to reality. Because right now he felt like he was floating in some otherworldly place where not a thing made sense. And it had nothing to do with the paraglider he'd just come off.

There was nothing he could do but to keep moving and get this meeting over with. Before he did something stupid. Like touch her to make sure she was really here.

Over coffee and some rather bad hospital sandwiches they went over the three cases and the ways in which each was similar and different. Two of the patients were from Brazil, including the last one. And one was from Honduras. They definitely met the parameters of exposure. All three of the babies had been born with microcephaly, one whose head was a third smaller than it should have been with some accompanying reflex problems. Another newborn was just under the norms. The third baby had clubbing of the hands and a cleft palate in addition to the microcephaly. There were pictures to accompany the reports.

Rafe's gut twinged a warning as he studied the images of the damage this virus could cause. One fateful encounter and someone's world changed forever. This time he wasn't thinking about Cassie, or even about Zika, but about his own childhood. One life gone, another life saved. It seemed like an even exchange when you laid it all out on paper. Only it wasn't. And yet that's exactly what had happened, due to a senseless act.

Hadn't he just celebrated that anniversary?

Celebrated wasn't the word he was looking for, but when one went out drinking and picking up women to help blot the pain of loss, it was the only term he could think of.

Only he'd never had to face any of those women again.

Until now.

And he could honestly say the experience was not one he cared to repeat. The hair tie in his pocket seemed to mock all his efforts. So much for forgetting.

"Any nearby hospitals reporting anything?"

Cassie glanced at Bonnie and Ms. Porter. "I have a colleague who works at Buena Vista who had a baby born with a cleft palate a week ago. No microcephaly in that case, though."

Alejandro spent most of his time over there, maybe he should give him a call. Although since his brother had found true love a few weeks ago and had adopted a special needs baby, he might be a little preoccupied with other things. No, Alejandro was nothing if not good at his job. But his specialty was pediatric transplants, not neonatal care, so it was a totally different field from what they were looking at here.

He tried not to think about the exact reasons his brother went into that field, because it brought up his own yearly vigil all over again.

It was his job to check every angle, though. "One of my brothers practices at Buena Vista, I'll give him a call. What's the name of your colleague?"

"Rebecca Stanton."

Her eyes had lost the defensive gleam they'd held moments earlier. The ring wasn't on her finger, so she and whoever she'd broken up with hadn't gotten back together.

No involvement. Remember?

The hospital administrator gave him a few phone numbers and names of people he could contact over at Buena Vista. "Is there anything else?" she asked.

"Not that I can think of at the moment. Are any of the patients still at the hospital?"

Cassie nodded. "Renato Silva. He developed some breathing issues, which we need to stabilize before releasing him."

"I'd like to examine him, if I could."

Ms. Porter went to the door. "I'll leave Dr. Larrobee to help you with that, then. Let me know if you have any further questions."

He shook hands with her and the infamous Bonnie, and waited until they left the room before saying anything else. "Bonnie, huh?"

"I know. I'm sorry for giving you a fake name. I just never dreamed…"

"You never dreamed you'd see me again."

"Actually, I didn't, or I wouldn't have…"

She wouldn't have what? Sat next to him at the bar? Spent the night with him?

"Isn't there a certain book that warns your sins shall find you out?"

A smile teased the corners of her mouth as color washed back into her face. "I think falsifying names were the least of our sins in that case."

Yes, they were. Thoughts that caused certain synapses in his brain to begin firing.

"I see you found another hair band."

Cassie's fingers went to the bun at the back of her head. "I did. You wouldn't happen to know where my other one went, would you?"

Any twinge of conscience he'd had over taking it

vanished at the way her voice lowered, the sultry edge he'd heard the night at the bar coming back.

"Not a clue."

Ha! If she knew the thing was about to burn a hole in his pocket, she'd probably kill him and leave his body in one of the supply closets.

It was one night, Rafe. Hardly worth mentioning.

Besides, he wasn't here to talk about hair ties or what they'd done. He was here to see if Zika was growing to epidemic proportions on their shoreline. "You haven't been to any of the countries involved, have you?"

She frowned as if confused by the question. "No. But it can be passed sexually, from what we're hearing."

"Yes. It can." Thank heavens they'd used condoms over the course of the night. "Your ex?"

She gave a short sound that could have been described as pained. "He barely steps out of his office, much less travels out of the country."

But they both knew that there were many diseases that could be spread down the line if there were multiple partners involved. And from what he'd sensed in Cassie at Mad Ron's a month ago, the man had done some straying.

Maybe she sensed what he was thinking because her chin tilted. "Do you want to go see Renato? Or not?"

There was a definite chill to her voice that hadn't been there a few moments earlier. He guessed she didn't take kindly to him mentioning the man she'd once been with.

"Yes." As she started to walk past him he touched

her arm. "Sorry for leaving you alone in the hotel. Did you make it home okay?"

Her brows came together and she motioned to the conference room. "Yes. I'm not quite destitute, as you can see. I didn't need your...contribution. I found it insulting, actually. I left it for the maid."

Contribution? Oh, the money.

"I didn't know what arrangements you'd made, and I was already late for work. I was afraid I might leave you stranded."

"I'm a big girl. I make it a point never to get myself into a situation that I can't get out of."

Rafe himself lived by that same motto, actually. He never let himself get embroiled in something that might require any emotional input. Or painful goodbyes. Even the job he'd chosen reflected that. Although he was an MD, he'd chosen epidemiology as his specialty. He was one step removed from being in contact with patients on a daily basis. A buffer zone that physicians didn't have. His role was more detached. And that's the way he'd chosen to live his life.

Deciding whether or not to give a hair tie back to its owner was as personal as he wanted to get. And even that was giving him some trouble.

But it was on a whole different level from deciding whether or not to disconnect life support. He'd vowed never to be put in that position again. So as long as the only people he allowed into his life were his brothers, he was good to go. Besides, he should be celebrating. Santi, the brother who had up and disappeared for a long period of time, had just come back into their lives.

He switched his thoughts back to Cassie and her

statement about not getting into situations she couldn't get out of.

"And yet you came to Mad Ron's because of one, didn't you?"

She gave a visible swallow, not answering immediately. And then she said, "Shall we go see Renato?"

He let the subject go, waiting for her to pass him, then he followed her down the hallway. The decision about what to do with the hair tie was made. It would stay in his pocket, and when he got home he would throw it away. And then he would most definitely forget about it.

And her.

Poor Renato had been poked and prodded so much since he'd been born, and yet the baby was taking everything much better than she expected him to.

Maybe even better than she was. Rafe had seemed so genuinely puzzled over her reaction to the money he'd left her that it had put her mind at ease. She'd been just about ready to forgive the lapse in judgment, and then he had to go and poke at what was still a very sore spot: her reasons for going to Mad Ron's in the first place. Her cheating fiancé, who she'd heard from exactly once since she'd caught him *in flagrante*, had asked for the ring back. Good thing she hadn't dumped it down the storm sewer outside the bar, like she'd thought about doing. She'd sent it via certified mail, gratified that his signature closed the final chapter on that relationship. Thank goodness she'd discovered who he really was now, rather than after they'd been married.

And yet it still hurt that someone she'd trusted

could do something like that to her. Especially since she didn't hand that trust out to just anyone. Tossed from foster home to foster home—she'd been seventeen before a kind couple had decided to adopt her—she'd learned very early on that most relationships didn't last.

So she'd avoided them altogether. Until Darrin. Who'd seemed like everything she could possibly dream of—steady, good-looking, career oriented. He was all those things. But he wasn't faithful.

Well, she was putting it all behind her. No more dating for a while.

Was that why she'd jumped into bed with the first available guy?

Ugh! No, Rafe was simply the punctuation mark that ended her relationship with her ex. From now on her job and her patients were what she was going to focus on. They were enough.

She forced her mind back to where the man in question was carefully listening to Renato's heart. "He has a slight murmur."

"Yes. He has a prolapsed mitral valve. And his breathing isn't quite where we want it to be yet, although it seemed fine right after birth."

"All Zika-related?" Rafe glanced up from the exam table.

"We're not sure. The mitral valve issue is common enough in the general population that we have no idea if it's due to the virus or if his valve would have been that way anyway."

"Any of the other cases include heart valves?"

What could seem like random anomalies, if taken on a case-by-case basis, could actually be part of a disease process if they occurred in clusters.

"Neither of the other two infants had heart involvement at all. But then again Renato doesn't have clubbed fingers or a cleft palate like one of the other patients." She hesitated. "And, honestly, if we don't see any more suspicious cases of birth defects, I will be ecstatic."

"So will the CDC. But we can't operate under that assumption."

"Any advances on the vaccine front?"

Rafe, who had handed her back her stethoscope, went to test the baby's grip reflex. Renato's fingers curled around the epidemiologist's thumb and held on.

A strange quiver went through her stomach when he didn't immediately tug free and move on to the other hand, but rather stood there, looking down at the baby. When he glanced up again, his eyes were dark, pupils large. "There are a couple of promising trials coming up. Hopefully we won't have very many more Renatos before a breakthrough is discovered."

Her throat tightened. "It's so terrible, isn't it? He had his whole life in front of him, and now..."

"I know."

Somehow, Cassie sensed Rafe really did know. She'd never found out exactly why he'd been drinking that night. He'd figured her reasons out by watching her take off her ring. But once they'd left the bar he hadn't been all that interested in holding lengthy conversations. He'd been too busy kissing her.

And more.

There it was again. That stream of heat that started in her head and rushed rapidly to the outer reaches of her body. If this was what hot flashes felt like, she wanted no part of them.

"Do you need anything else?"

"I think I have enough for this visit."

This visit? As in there would be more? She had been counting on this being a chance meeting. A fluke. Kind of like Mad Ron's had been.

Rafe eased his thumb from the baby's grip and carefully picked him up, tucking him under his chin and holding him close for a moment.

The warm flush grew despite her best efforts. Some woman was going to be lucky to get him. He was drop-dead gorgeous, and she could tell babies held a special place in his heart.

Except she had a feeling she wasn't the first woman he'd picked up in Mad Ron's. And she probably wouldn't be the last. That should tell her right there that he wasn't a one-woman kind of man.

Well, neither was her ex.

Yes, and it was a good thing she'd thought of Darrin, because it was enough to put her back on the straight and narrow. Maybe she could find a convent that would take her in.

As ridiculous as that was, the thought made her stop. She didn't want to join an actual cloister or abandon the human race entirely, but couldn't she turn her heart into one? She'd let one man in and it had been a disaster. One she didn't want to repeat. If she could figure out how to fashion her life into an impenetrable fortress, she could stand in its turret and rain arrows down on any man who ventured too close.

Like Rafe?

No, he'd been a one-night stand, a fling, nothing more, nothing less.

Liar, liar...

Rafe's amused words during their meeting in the conference room came back to haunt her.

She may have been lying about her name, but she wasn't lying about the one-night-stand part. This man was dangerous. The less she had to do with him, the better.

Maybe she should make things as plain as she could for him—and for her—to make sure his references to "next time" were just idle talk. Especially if the Zika thing was actually a "thing" and they really did need to work together more than this one time.

She hesitated.

Come on, Cassie. Embarrassment is a small price to pay to make sure things don't get more awkward than they already are.

"Can I say something?"

He glanced up, the baby still tucked close. "Of course."

"That night at the bar was… Well, I wasn't myself. I don't want you to get the wrong idea. I'm not looking for a relationship."

A frown appeared. "You made that pretty obvious when you came in with an engagement ring and handed me a fake name. But, just for the record, I agree with you. It was a one-time thing. Not to be repeated."

The quick stab of pain was unexpected, but necessary. So were her next words. "As long as we're both clear. And I'd appreciate your keeping what happened between us."

"I wasn't planning on writing any journal articles or using you as a reference on my résumé, if that's what you're worried about." This time his voice was a little harder than it had been. She ignored it.

"Great. It sounds like we're on the same page. Now, I'll take the baby, if you're done examining him."

As he handed Renato back to her, Cassie breathed an inner oath to herself. As of this moment she was going to stay true to her word and watch her Ps and Qs with this man.

Although, if she were very, very lucky, there would be no more Zika cases at her hospital, and no reason to see a certain epidemiologist ever, ever again.

CHAPTER TWO

BONNIE CORNERED CASSIE in the cafeteria a few hours later, dropping into the seat across from her. "So what was that all about?"

Her friend was everything she wasn't. With untamed red hair and a personality to match, they were about as opposite as they could be. And yet they'd been friends since elementary school—their friendship the only stable thing in an unstable childhood. Bonnie had dared her to do some outrageous stunts during the course of their lives, most of which had been turned down with a shocked "Are you insane?" Her friend was the one, though, who had talked her into going to medical school, saying she had the "smarts." Working at the same hospital with her was both fun and, at times, extremely scary. Like right now.

She decided to play it cool. "What was what, Bon?"

"Um…that CDC man thinking I was you? He may have said my name, but he was staring right at you."

"Was he?" Hadn't she just asked Rafe not to mention their little tryst? She gulped. Well, he probably didn't have someone like Bonnie grilling him. He seemed like a loner.

Her friend propped her arms on the table, leaning

forward and giving her a dark glare. "If you could have seen the look on your face when he said he'd already met 'Bonnie' you wouldn't bother using that innocent act on me. I can see right through it. What happened?"

"I picked him up at a bar." Yep. She would just keep what had happened to herself. She gave an internal eye-roll.

"You...*what*?"

Cassie couldn't prevent a laugh. "Okay, so if your face looks anything like you say mine did, then I'm in big trouble. Close your mouth, silly."

Bonnie obliged with an audible click of her teeth. "Okay, just let me wrap my head around this for a second. I cannot imagine you picking up *anyone*. Especially so soon after Darrin. Where did you go?"

"Mad Ron's. And it was the same night as the break-up actually. I yanked the ring off on the way through the door."

"Wow. Just wow." Her friend snagged a grape from Cassie's plate and looked at her with something akin to envy. "This is probably the only impulsive thing you'll do in your entire life, and I didn't even get an invitation. Or a video."

"Um... I don't think you would have wanted an invitation, and certainly not a video, for part of it." Most of it, actually. Her friend knew how to keep a secret so there was no harm in letting her in on it. Right?

Bonnie popped the fruit into her mouth, chewing for a few seconds. "Maybe not. But I would have loved to have been a fly on the wall. That still doesn't answer my question, though. Why did he think I was—" She stopped, eyes widening. "Oh, wait. You gave him my name. You...you *impersonated* me."

"I didn't impersonate you. I would have had to wear a wig and get a personality transplant to do that. I just didn't think I'd ever see the man again. And if he turned out to be some kind of weird stalker…"

"Oh, I see. You'd rather sic the crazed stalker on your best friend. Although, after looking at him, I might not have minded. As long as he offered sex. And lots of it."

"Bonnie! I meant the psychopath kind of stalker." Cassie laughed again, partly to cover her embarrassment. Because he had offered sex. Lots of it, as her friend had said. "If he'd turned out to be some kind of weirdo, I knew you'd make short work of him with that jujitsu stuff you do."

Bonnie had actually had to get them out of a tricky situation a few years back—a carjacker had tried to come through her open window. The result had been a concussion for the jerk when her friend had somehow managed to turn her body enough to land a sharp kick to his head. Through the window!

She hadn't really thought Rafe would turn out to be a psychopath, she just hadn't wanted him to try calling her for another date, if he'd gotten the wrong impression about what she'd wanted from him.

Not that she was proud of herself for going the hot-sex-and-nothing-else route, but she'd been livid and crushed and horrified when she'd discovered Darrin's infidelity. She'd wanted revenge. And to forget.

Rafe had helped her to forget that night, that was for sure. Except she couldn't quite scrub him from her mind as easily as she'd thought she'd be able to, despite her words to the contrary. And the image of him holding Renato's tiny form to his chest…

Her food suddenly looked very unappetizing. Queasy-making, actually. She shoved her tray over to Bonnie when the nurse picked up another grape. "You can have it. I'm not hungry all of a sudden."

Bonnie tilted her head, concern coming into her eyes. "Hey, don't get upset. I hereby give you permission to use my name anytime you want. I think it's kind of funny, actually. And if Dr. Tall, Dark and Sexy ever wants a threesome..."

Before Cassie could express her shock or deny that she was ever going to sleep with the man again, her friend held up a hand. "I'm kidding. Are you sure you're okay? You normally get my cracked sense of humor."

Yes she did, and Cassie wasn't sure why it was striking such a weird chord today. "Sorry, it's just been a hard month."

"Maybe we should go out and do something fun. Take your mind off of things."

The oily sensation in her tummy grew, forcing her to swallow. Bonnie had a point, though. She'd let herself dwell on her troubles for far too long. Maybe that was the source of her sour stomach and even sourer disposition. "Maybe we should. When is your next day off?"

"I'm off on Friday."

"Hmm... I have to work the morning shift, but I get off at three—would that work?"

"Absolutely." Bonnie wiggled her eyebrows. "What I have in mind is a night-time activity, anyway."

"Bonnie..." The note of warning she'd injected into her voice did nothing to deter her friend.

"What? Don't most people eat *dinner* at night?"

"You're impossible."

"Yep. That's why you lubs me." She picked up Cassie's fork and dug into the tuna salad over lettuce. "Thanks for lunch, by the way."

"Not a problem. So Friday dinner?"

"Yep. Maybe we could swap names for the night and pick up some hotties. Do a little role-playing and compare notes."

Cassie crumpled up her napkin and threw it at her friend. "Forget it. Once has been more than enough. I'll leave the pickup lines to you." Not that Bonnie did anything too risky. She just liked to have a good time.

Friday was two days away, so that should give her time to throw off whatever weirdness was going on with her system and get back to being her normal perky self.

Well, perky probably wasn't a word she'd use to describe herself—that was Bonnie's domain. But she could at least start getting back some of her equilibrium. Between Darrin and that night with Rafe, she had been off balance for weeks. It was time to move forward and forget about all of that.

"See you on Friday, then."

She stood and then stopped when Bonnie pointed the knife she was using at her. "By the way, if that hunky epidemiologist contacts you again, I want to be the first to know."

Well, Rafe had contacted her again, but Cassie could wait until her dinner date with Bonnie to tell her about it. Cynthia Porter had requested that she pay a visit to Buena Vista Hospital on the other side of town. Cassie, with her big mouth, had mentioned her colleague over there, and Ms. Porter had taken that as a willingness to go over there after her shift. And guess who she got to go with.

None other than the epidemiologist himself. It should have been a piece of cake, right?

Wrong. Because she was now trapped in a car with him, and that yummy, totally manly scent was surrounding her and threatening to cut off her breathing altogether. It also triggered a memory of a very different time when she'd shared a space with him. A very intimate space.

A shiver went through her.

"Too cool?" He'd evidently seen her reaction, because his fingers moved to the climate-control system of the vehicle.

Pull yourself together, Cassie. You had a brief interlude with the man. It meant absolutely nothing.

So why was sitting next to him doing a number on her?

"I'm fine. I'm not exactly sure how I can help you."

"I'd like to compare notes with some of the folks at Buena Vista and see if there are any similarities between your cases and theirs. You know your patients better than anyone."

Which was why she had three sets of case files perched on her lap. She'd had to call the parents of each of the affected babies and ask if they could share information with the other hospital. All of them had agreed, Renato's mom saying she wanted to do anything she could to make sure this didn't happen to anyone else's child.

And that had been the deciding factor in Cassie going. She too was willing to do anything she could to help prevent Zika from harming any more babies.

Spending a few additional hours in Rafe's company was a small price to pay.

That didn't make it any less uncomfortable, though.

"Did you find out if there are any cases over there?"

"I checked with my brother…" he glanced over at her, his brown eyes skimming her face "…and he made a few calls. The prenatal and maternity departments came up with a couple of red flags."

"Really?" That surprised her a little. She would have expected more cases at Seaside, since it was a public hospital. Immigrants, both papered and unpapered, tended to favor her hospital, since it made more provisions as far as translators and government resources went. Neighborhoods in Miami tended to form based on language and culture, which was how places like little Havana had come into being. It helped make the transition to the United States a little less painful for newcomers.

"Is it my imagination or am I'm hearing something behind that 'really?'"

"We just tend to get more of the patients who might have come from affected regions than Buena Vista."

"My family is from Heliconia. California has reported two cases of Zika-related microcephaly in newborns whose mothers recently emigrated from my home country."

His home country. The low murmur of Spanish from a month ago trickled through her memory and sent heat sloshing through her belly. She did her best to stem the tide.

"Do your parents live nearby?"

There was a pause and Rafe's hands tightened on

the wheel, before loosening his grip. "My three brothers do."

That was weird. She hadn't asked about his brothers. "So you came to the States as adults?" He didn't
have an accent that she could detect, but his Spanish
had been flawless.

"Dante and I were children when we arrived here.
My other two brothers were born in this country."

So his parents had emigrated from Heliconia. And
yet he still hadn't mentioned them. Not once. Had they
moved back home?

"Are you hearing anything about Zika from relatives in Heliconia?" She shouldn't be asking, and she
knew that her digging was not entirely professional.
She was curious about him and his brothers and their
reasons for moving to the States.

"No."

And that short answer put her in her place. He didn't
want any more personal questions. Okay, that was fine.

He stared at the road for several more seconds and
then took a deep breath, blowing it out. "Sorry. My
parents are both dead. They've been gone since Dante
and I were eighteen."

Both of them? Shock wheeled through her. They
must have been killed in a car accident or something.

"I'm so sorry. They died here in Miami?"

"Yes. My father passed away at Buena Vista, in
fact."

There was a terrible note in his voice that she
couldn't decipher. She swallowed, not wanting to think
about what he and his brothers must have gone through.
And, really, it was none of her business. She decided
to change to a less intrusive topic.

"You and Dante are the same age? You're twins?"

"Yes. Fraternal ones. Alejandro and Santi are obviously younger." He smiled, a flicker of what might have been relief in his brown eyes as he glanced over. "And they're not twins, before you ask."

She smiled back. "That certainly would have made life interesting. So your brothers all live in the area, you said."

"They do now."

"But not before."

"Three of us did. Santi just recently…returned." He rubbed the back of his neck. "What about you? Any brothers or sisters?"

"No." She hesitated, but decided not tell him that her biological parents had both been drug addicts who'd been in and out of prison. Or that she'd been shuffled from one foster home to another during her childhood, until finally her parents had fallen off the radar altogether.

None of that mattered, though. The people she cared about the most—the ones she considered her *real* parents—had taken her in as a teenager and had given her their last name.

She decided to acknowledge that fact. "My parents live pretty close to here. My dad is a marine biologist."

"You grew up on the water, then."

"Not really." Yet another thing that would be hard to explain, since she hadn't actually grown up with her adoptive parents. "I'm not crazy about the ocean. Too many things swimming down there. I think my dad's stories about what he's seen on some of his dive trips had the opposite effect to what he'd hoped. I think he secretly envisioned me following in his footsteps."

"But you didn't." Rafe stopped for a red light. "You became a neonatologist instead."

She'd often wondered if maybe that was so she could help babies get off to a better start than she'd had.

"I did." She paused, thinking through her answer. "I would have had a baby brother, if he'd survived. He was stillborn." Her mom's one and only pregnancy had happened right after they'd adopted her. It had taken a lot of reassurance to make her believe that they would still want her, even if they had ten other children. It hadn't happened, and complications had caused the doctors to recommend a hysterectomy soon after the baby was born.

That made him look. "I'm sorry. My mom had several miscarriages. It was why she and my dad decided to emigrate to the States. She was pregnant with Santi and was worried things would go wrong again. So they chanced getting passage on a small boat. They made it. And Santi was obviously fine."

Small boat. Did he mean…? Either way, they'd made it, and Rafe's brother had survived. "What do they do? Your brothers, that is."

The light changed back and the vehicle slid smoothly into traffic. "Dante is a neurosurgeon. Alejandro is a pediatric transplant surgeon, and Santi is a paramedic."

That stopped her for a second.

"You're all in medicine?" How often did siblings go into such similar fields?

"Yes."

He didn't offer up any more explanation than that, although she got the idea there was more to the story. Besides, there was Buena Vista just ahead on the right. Her queasiness from a couple of days ago hadn't quite given up. If it held on any longer, she would need to get it checked out. She didn't want to pass anything on to her tiny charges. She'd been super-diligent about hand washing and making sure she wore gloves and a mask with any of her more vulnerable patients, like Renato.

As he pulled in and found a spot for his car in the covered lot, she was struck by how different Buena Vista was from Seaside. The building was modern, the landscaping well planned and tended. Not that Seaside was ugly, by any means. They provided first-class care for their patients, but since it was a public hospital they couldn't always afford the things that private facilities like this one offered.

Turning off the engine of his vehicle, he dropped his keys and smartphone into the pocket of his sport coat. Only then did he shift his upper body around to face her. Everything inside of her went wonky when his fingers touched the back of her hand, his eyes searching hers. For a brief second she thought he was going to kiss her.

Would she let him? As if her body had already made its decision, her teeth came down and pinned her lower lip.

"Cassie?"

"Yes?" The breathlessness in her voice made her cringe. She sat up straighter, hoping he hadn't heard it.

"If we happen to see one of my brothers in there, and with the way my luck runs we will, can I ask you not to say anything about our conversation just now?"

The tingling in her midsection came to an abrupt halt.

"Our conversation?"

"About my parents."

She would have expected him to ask her to keep the night they'd spent together quiet, just like she'd asked him at Seaside that day. Instead, he'd evidently said something on their ride over that he hadn't meant to. Something he didn't tell many other people. His mom's miscarriages? Their trip over on the boat? Whatever it was, he needed some kind of reassurance. Reassurance she was suddenly more than happy to supply.

With his hand still covering hers, and the warmth of his skin penetrating the chill from the air-conditioner, she gave him what he wanted. "I won't say a word, Rafe. To anyone."

Why had he mentioned his parents? Not that he had, really. But he'd said much more than he'd intended to. Cassie seemed to invite confidences and a whole lot more. Walking out of the meeting an hour later with Cassie not far behind him, he swore softly when he spied two of his brothers in conversation over by the emergency entrance. Just when he'd begun to hope they might get out of there without seeing either of them. Not happening, evidently. Santi must have just come off a run. The pair waved him over.

"Alejandro tried to call your cell a little while ago, but didn't get an answer. He figured you must be in the air somewhere." Santi gave him a quick slap on the shoulder, looking past him. "Who's this?"

Perfect. Paragliding would have been the preferable option to this. He would have to run into the two Valentino brothers who had found "true love." Santi with Saoirse Murphy and Alejandro with Kiri Bhardwaj. Why couldn't it have been the still-single Dante?

"This is Dr. Larrobee. She's here on a consult with

the neonatal department. It's to do with the possible Zika cases I called Alejandro about."

"Oh, right." Alejandro leaned over and shook Cassie's hand. "Are you worried about Buena Vista being affected?"

Santi took his turn greeting Cassie, while Rafe waited.

"It could hit anywhere. There were a couple of iffy cases, so we met with some of the doctors to compare notes. We're hoping for the best but expecting the worst." He shoved his hands in his pockets.

"Really. Let us know what you turn up." Santi gave Alejandro a glance. "That reminds me. Carmelita wants us all to meet up at the bodega in a little while."

His brother cocked his head. "She does?"

"Yes, we haven't gone over the inventory lists since..." He smiled. "Well, you and I have been a little busy with weddings and other things over the past few months. The meeting shouldn't take long."

Oh, brother. He could always tell them he had other plans, but it would be a lie. And for some reason he didn't want Cassie to think he had a date. Or, worse, for his brothers to think he was going out with Cassie.

"We both got married recently," Alejandro explained, as if reading his mind.

Cassie smiled. "Congratulations."

"I'm a lucky man."

Rafe glanced at his brother with concern. Had there been a little catch in his voice when he'd said that? Alejandro had had a scare a month ago and had undergone a heart cath when scar tissue had blocked the organ. But he seemed fine right now. And then there was his newly adopted son, little Gervaso...

Time to break up this party, though, before his brothers got any strange ideas. "I have no idea what Kiri sees in you, oh ugly one."

It was a running joke between the four of them, each claiming the other brothers were all the "ugly ones."

"Rafe!" Cassie's chiding voice came from beside him.

"It's okay," Alejandro said. "He knows *he's* actually the ugly one. And old to boot."

Except now both of his brothers were showing renewed interest in Cassie. Maybe because she'd called him by his first name, rather than giving him his professional title.

Perfect.

"When exactly does Carmelita want us to meet?"

"How about now? She is always complaining about how hard it is to round all of us up." Santi had his phone in his hand.

"Cassie rode over here with me. I'm sure she isn't interested in going."

"The bodega closes in a half hour." Santi glanced at Cassie. "Do you mind stopping there for a few minutes? Like I said, it shouldn't take long."

"Alejandro, don't you have a baby to check on?" Rafe's jaw tightened as he tried to deflect the conversation to the heart transplant baby his brother and Kiri had adopted.

"Gervaso is doing great." The pride in his brother's voice was evident when he spoke of his new son. Rafe had to admit both Alejandro and Santi seemed happier than he'd ever seen them.

Cassie touched his arm. "A quick side trip won't

hold me up at all, as long as you can have me back at Seaside by four."

"Are you going on duty again?"

"No, I'm having dinner with a friend."

A friend?

It was none of his business who she saw. But if it was that oaf who'd hurt her…

Hold up, Rafe. It has nothing to do with you.

It did make his mind up, though. "If you're sure?"

"I am. I don't think I've actually been to a bodega before. What is it exactly?"

He waited for one of his brothers to explain, but when they both remained miraculously silent he answered. "It's kind of a convenience store with a Latino flair. They sell tomatillos and specialty spices. My parents founded it. It came about because they missed some of the foods from their homeland. It snowballed as they imported stuff for other Heliconians. So the bodega was born. It's been in the family ever since."

"Wow. I guess I have noticed them, I just never knew what they were called. You all run it together?"

"We do, with the help of Carmelita."

"She's a friend of the family," Rafe explained. "A kind of *tia*—aunt. She manages the place for us now. We haven't had an official meeting in a few weeks, though, and I guess she's wondering what happened to us."

It might have been easier to just sell the small mom-and-pop store. After all, the bodega contained some terrible memories. But it was also something his parents had cherished. They'd worked hard to carve a place for themselves in the community. The bodega had been their pride and joy. None of the brothers had

had the heart to close it down or sell it, although that might have been less painful in the long run.

"I'd love to see it."

Alejandro drew his keys from one of his pockets. "I guess that's it, then. We meet over there in around fifteen minutes?"

"Do I have a choice?" Rafe asked.

"No." Santi threw a smile over his shoulder. "Don't worry. It'll be quick and painless."

Somehow Rafe doubted that. "Okay, we'll see you there."

Maybe by the time they arrived at the bodega he and Cassie would have figured out what their next step should be.

Not *their* next step. His. Because if he could help it, he was going to investigate the Zika scare on his own from here on out.

As for the bodega meeting, it was no biggie. His brothers would never guess the truth: that he'd spent one unforgettable, incredible night with Dr. Cassandra Larrobee, neonatologist.

And once he and Cassie went their separate ways, everything would go back to the way it had been before they'd met.

At least, Rafe sincerely hoped it would.

CHAPTER THREE

CASSIE WAS BEGINNING to feel sorry she'd made that call to the CDC.

No, she wasn't. The Renatos of the world deserved to have someone fight for them. To make sure that what happened to him and the others didn't turn into an epidemic. If she could help, she would. Even if it meant meeting Rafe and his brothers, and going to his parents' shop.

In the end it wasn't that big of a deal.

Back in the car, next to Rafe, she tried not to dwell on the fact that she was a little bit nervous to be included in their meet up. No, she wasn't "included." She was only coming because it was easier than dropping her off at home.

Rafe, Santi and Alejandro all had stunning good looks with dark hair and even darker eyes. The sibling she hadn't met—Dante—was probably just as big a hottie as the rest of them. Ugly, her ass. They could only joke like that because the brothers were the antithesis of homely. Anyone seeing them together would have realized immediately they were brothers. Any woman in her right mind would be a little over-awed by them.

It had nothing to do with Rafe or what they'd done.

"How far away is the bodega?"

"Just a few more blocks." He cut a glance her way. "Having second thoughts?"

Yep, and it was definitely time to put some distance between them. He was beginning to read her far too easily, unless it had just been a lucky guess. She wasn't going to admit that for the world, though.

"I'll just look around the store while you guys talk, if that's okay."

"Sure. There are a lot of interesting items there."

"I bet." She had a thought. "Nothing illegal, though, right?" Drugs were a huge problem in Miami. She wanted to make sure she wasn't getting involved in something she would regret.

Not that she was getting involved. She just needed to be cautious, a trait she'd somehow misplaced when dealing with Rafe. But she'd better locate that sucker, pronto.

Her stomach shifted inside her, giving a little squeeze to remind her that it was still there.

"Do we look like a gang of drug dealers?"

Stranger things had happened. But he was right. There'd been no hint of drugs during the night they'd spent together. Just a few drinks. "No. Sorry."

He gave her a lopsided smile. "It's okay. I'm sure we can look like quite the crew when you get us all together."

Yes, they did. And that was half the problem.

"So there's Santi, Alejandro, you and...was it Dante?"

"Yes."

"Wow."

He cocked a brow at her. "What does that mean?"

"Your names are just all so…"

Sexy. There. She could admit it to herself, even if she would never dare to say it to Rafe or his brothers.

"All what?"

"Latino sounding."

He laughed, the deep sound washing over her and making a smile come to her lips. "Well, since we are actually from Scandinavia…"

"Very funny. Is Rafe short for something?"

"Rafael." He pronounced it with that smooth Spanish roll of the *R* that sent heat pulsing through her chest, belly…and beyond. She'd loved listening to him as they'd made love. The words had been dark. And mysterious. Hinting at all kinds of decadent things.

Whoa! Time to slow down those thoughts. Or she was going to have to move the vent so it was blowing cold air directly on her face. She cleared her throat.

"It must have been neat, growing up with siblings."

There. That was a safe enough topic. Her only siblings had been transient, the relationships only lasting as long as whatever home she'd been in at the time.

A shadow crossed his face. "Yes. My mom could keep us all in line with just a look." He shrugged. "You wouldn't know it by looking at any of us now."

He pulled up to a corner, where a colorful sign hung over a small hole-in-the-wall store.

Valentino's.

"Here we are."

She stared at the building with its floral-tiled façade and cobblestone sidewalk. "It's so quaint. I love it!"

"Wait until you see inside." He parked behind a

motorcycle. "Looks like everyone's already here. Are you sure you want to go in?"

It didn't sound like Rafe was all that thrilled with the idea. But she wanted to see it, although she wasn't sure why. She'd grown up in Miami, but she'd never really gotten a chance to be immersed in another culture. She'd known plenty of Brazilians and Cubans, and could speak passable Spanish and Portuguese, but most of her knowledge consisted of tangible things like black beans and rice and fried plantains.

"I really do. I promise I won't intrude on your family time. Unless you're going to have fifty relatives in there, then it might be a little hard to avoid bumping into one another."

His mouth tipped up slightly. "Hopefully it'll just be me, my brothers and Carmelita."

"Who else would there be?"

"It doesn't matter. Shall we?" He got out of the car, circling the hood as if coming around to open her door. She beat him to it, throwing it wide and stepping onto the curb.

She felt a little out of place in her hospital attire, especially since Rafe had on street clothes. She'd shopped in her scrubs before, though, so why did she suddenly care how she looked?

Reaching back, she tightened her ponytail holder and straightened her shoulders. It was fine.

When they ducked inside the tiny store, she found it packed to the gills with strange-looking merchandise. Fascinated, she fingered the Spanish language labels. It wasn't just food that the place carried. There were tall glass votives sporting the image of the Virgin Mary on a long shelf toward the front of the store, as well as packages with pictures of hammocks on the front.

Rafe murmured, *"Dios.* They're here already."

Why did he make that sound like a bad thing?

She glanced up to see that his brothers and a woman were standing by the front counter, talking. And watching. One of them jerked his head to motion Rafe over. Except that when he started to move toward them, the brother she hadn't met shook his head. "Bring her with you. And tell me you're not following in the footsteps of these *feos.*"

She wasn't sure what the man was talking about but, whatever it was, Rafe wasn't happy about it. His whole body tensed. *"Hermano, no comienza conmigo."*

Had he forgotten that she understood Spanish or did he just not care? Because that "Brother, don't start with me" had been full of irritation. But about what?

"I'm not starting anything. Are you?"

Rafe just shook his head. "Cassie, this jerk is obviously Dante. Actually, they're all jerks. And ugly, to boot. Except for Carmelita. She keeps us on the straight and narrow. At least she tries."

"It is not easy, you boys are a handful." The woman's Spanish accent—much thicker than Rafe's or any of the other brothers'—was charming.

Cassie smiled. "I can well imagine." They might be a handful, but they were the best-looking bunch of brothers she'd seen in a long time, despite Rafe's claims to the contrary. And they dwarfed the manager, who stood in the middle of the group like a proud little mother hen. If you'd plopped the Valentino brothers together someplace like Mad Ron's, they would have easily been mistaken for bouncers.

"Will you not introduce me, Rafael? Manners. Manners." The woman reached out and gave Cassie a light kiss on the cheek.

Rafe's face infused with color. "Of course. This is Dr. Cassandra Larrobee. We just came from a *business meeting* at Buena Vista Hospital about *la Zika*." He glared at his brothers, addressing them as a group. "So, why are we here again?"

"No particular reason." Santi looked the picture of cunning innocence. "But since you and Dante are the Elders, we thought you should have some input on the...er...*tomatillos*."

What? She could have sworn that the other man had said there was an issue with the bodega's inventory when they'd been at the hospital.

Dante frowned. "Knock it off with the 'Elders' business. And tomatillos? You've got to be kidding me."

"Boys," Carmelita said. "I have not seen all of you together for a while, so if it must be over a can of tomatillos, *bueno*. It also gives me a chance to meet Rafe's—"

A cry interrupted her. "Help! Please help me!"

Cassie looked round to see a woman staggering into the doorway of the bodega, a huge splash of what looked like red paint staining her shirt. A maternity top. And her stomach was...

That wasn't paint. It was blood!

The room erupted in chaos, all of the brothers rushing toward her. Santi grabbed the woman just as her knees buckled. Carmelita was already ripping a lounge cushion from a nearby rack, tossing it onto the floor while Santi and Rafe helped the woman down onto it.

Rafe's face was pale as he called to Dante, "Lock the door. Now."

Had she been shot? Cassie hadn't heard anything, but the blood was in the wrong spot for it to be labor, although the woman looked like she was full term.

Alejandro was already on the phone, speaking with someone. "I don't know for sure, but we need police and the EMTs down here."

"Can you tell us what happened?" Santi eased the woman's shirt up over her swollen belly. Cassie was horrified to see what looked like a deep gash to the left of her bellybutton. It had to be six inches long.

"She...she wanted my baby. Said I didn't deserve..." The words were interrupted by a long scream, as the woman's abdomen visibly tightened. She was in labor!

A gush of blood spurted from the wound as the muscles contracted. Dante rushed to another rack, coming back with several packages of gauze. Ripping into one of them, he handed a huge wad of the bandaging material to Santi, who knelt and held it against the wound, trying to staunch the bleeding.

The men looked at each other just as Cassie figured it out: someone had tried to cut the baby out of her womb.

"Mierda!" Santi pushed harder. "Where are the police?"

Cassie knelt beside the woman's head, trying to coach her through the rest of the contraction as she gave a pitiful moan. Who could have done such a thing?

If help didn't come soon, they would be in danger of losing both mother and baby.

Rafe was on another phone. He squatted down beside them, glancing at Cassie with worried eyes. Then he leaned in to whisper to her, "They want you to ask her if she knows the name of who did this."

"Now?" The only thing she cared about at the moment was helping the victims.

He nodded.

Damn. She suddenly knew why they wanted the information right now. If the woman died without naming her attacker, the police would have little to go on. She swallowed hard, tears coming to her eyes as she smoothed a few locks of hair from the young woman's sweaty face. With her dark hair pulled back in a ponytail and yoga pants, she looked to be in her early twenties. So young. She could have been headed anywhere, happily going about her life. And then something like this happened. It was unfathomable. She tried to get the woman's attention.

The contraction had subsided, the grip on her hand easing, although she was still moaning in pain. "What's your name?"

"S-Samantha." The fear was evident as her hands went to her abdomen and came away slick with blood despite the pressure on the wound. "Am I going to die? Is my baby…?"

The lines in Santi's face were tight. "The baby is moving, Samantha. We're all doctors, and Cassandra is a neonatologist who specializes in newborns. You're in good hands. And the ambulance should be here any minute."

"He's right. One of us will be with you the whole way." A nudge from Rafe reminded her what she was supposed to ask. "Samantha, I know this is hard, but do you know who did this to you?"

A sob erupted from her throat and she nodded. "Yes.

It…" The words faded away as her head went back, another hoarse cry filling the air. "Ahhhhh…it's starting again."

Another contraction. Even as she said it, Santi pressed down with the bandaging material, putting strong pressure on the wound. It was soaked within seconds. "Dante, I need another package."

His brother was already on it, opening one and giving him a fresh bundle of gauze.

No gloves. None of them were using any. But then again there hadn't been time to do anything except to leap into emergency mode.

"Breathe." Cassie murmured instructions, glancing up at Rafe. His face was pasty white and he looked like he was going to be sick. She could understand a normal person getting queasy, but Rafe was not only an epidemiologist, he had a medical degree. And yet he looked like he was staring into the face of death. She sent him a questioning glance, but instead of it pushing him into action he stood up and took a few steps back, looking down on the scene, the phone still to his ear. He said something to what must be the police officer on the other end.

Alejandro, who was standing nearby, put a hand on his shoulder, giving it a squeeze. If anything, the gesture just made things worse, judging from the skin stretched tightly across Rafe's cheekbones.

Cassie couldn't dwell on that, so she focused her attention on keeping the woman actively breathing through the contraction, watching for signs that she was going to pass out from blood loss.

The contraction eased and Samantha stiffened. "I think I'm going to be…"

Anticipating her words, Cassie tipped the woman's head to the right just as she vomited bile. No blood. A weird thing to be thankful for, but she was. If Santi had been telling the truth about the baby's movements, it was another thing the young woman could hold onto. Anything to give her hope.

Where was that ambulance? She couldn't even hear sirens yet. But in a city this size there could be all kinds of holdups, and the bodega was kind of out of the way, from what she'd seen as they'd driven over. The traffic snarls in the narrower streets of the neighborhoods could also be an issue.

Dante also moved to Rafe's side. *"Estás bien, hermano?"*

She and Alejandro weren't the only ones who'd noticed something odd about the epidemiologist's behavior. Maybe he wasn't used to being on this side of the scene when it came to emergencies. He dealt more in prevention and discovery, but he was a doctor, so surely…

Rafe waved them both off with a brusque, "I'm fine." But anyone could see the man wasn't fine. None of them were. Samantha was fighting for her life and for that of her baby. It was a horrific thing for anyone to witness.

The pile of blood-soaked gauze had grown to a small mound on the floor.

A faint siren sounded in the distance.

Thank God!

Samantha heard it as well. She tightened her grip on Cassie's hand. "My fiancé's old girlfriend, her name is…" her eyelids fluttered and then came open again as she struggled to focus "…Bridget…"

The woman's voice faded away.

"Samantha? Stay with us. Can you hear me?" She leaned closer, trying to rouse her again.

Dante knelt and took her pulse. "She's getting weaker."

"I hear the ambulance now," Cassie said.

"Rafe or Dante, can one of you take my place, while I catch the squad outside? I want to fill them in."

Dante glanced up at Rafe, who held the phone to his ear before moving to Santi's spot. Was he still relaying information? Or was he too paralyzed by the way things were playing out?

Cassie was upset too, nauseous, in fact. She should be irritated by Rafe's detached reaction to the situation, but instead she was worried.

A professional reaction, nothing more.

Something about the way Dante had asked if he was okay struck a chord. She knew of cases where relatives facing terrible tragedies pulled together and comforted each other.

But this woman was a complete stranger, wasn't she?

Hadn't Rafe said his mother had suffered several miscarriages—had risked traveling to the United States for just such a reason? Maybe seeing all this blood from a pregnant woman had triggered some distant memory that he just couldn't face. He'd asked her not to mention their conversation to his brothers but did that even have anything to do with this? None of the rest of them appeared as distraught as Rafe was.

It didn't matter. What did was the woman currently fighting for her life. She forced her attention back to Samantha, calling her name and trying to get her to respond. It had no effect. Samantha's body, however, was on an unstoppable course. Her contractions were closer together. Stronger. Less than two minutes apart now. If they didn't get her to a hospital soon…

Santi came back in with two EMT workers, one wheeling a stretcher and the other carrying what looked like a tackle box of equipment. With three of the brothers belting out instructions, an IV was soon started and Samantha was lifted onto the gurney. "Where's she going?"

"Buena Vista is closer."

Alejandro stepped up. "That's more my turf, I'll ride in with her."

"Are you sure you're up to it?" Dante asked.

"Yeah. I'll be fine."

Cassie wasn't sure what that was about, but as long as they got the patient into that ambulance, she didn't care which one of the brothers rode with her.

The woman hadn't been carrying a purse when she'd lurched into the bodega. Cassie probably should have thought to ask, but in the ensuing emergency and with Rafe trying to get the name of whoever had done this to her, she hadn't even thought to get Samantha's full name, or ask the names of her fiancé and family. And now she was unconscious.

Her throat tightened. Even though she considered herself a hardened professional, it was difficult to keep her eyes from moistening. Maybe that's where Rafe's thoughts were too. Maybe his emotions had gotten the better of him.

One EMT held the IV bag while the other wheeled the gurney out the door. Going alongside them was Alejandro—now gloved up, thanks to one of the emergency workers handing him some. He'd taken over Santi's job of maintaining pressure on the woman's abdomen as they went over the curb and paused at the back of the truck. Pushing the stretcher against the vehicle, the wheels retracted. Alejandro ducked inside with the other EMT. Then the doors slammed and the second emergency worker leaped inside the cab of the truck.

They were off, sirens blaring as they dodged in and out of traffic on the narrow street.

Cassie sent up a silent prayer. Hopefully Samantha and the baby would both survive. She had no idea how far along she even was, but it had looked like late pregnancy. She put in an addendum to her silent request: for Samantha to be far enough along that the baby would survive the trauma and the birth.

There was no way to stop the labor at this point, not with the contractions as close together as they were. In fact, it was almost certain the doctors would deliver the baby by C-section in an effort to save the life of the mother.

Taking a shaking breath, she went back inside the bodega. The three brothers who'd stayed behind were huddled together, along with Carmelita.

Cassie went from feeling like she was part of a team working together to feeling very much like an outsider. And although it was a familiar feeling, she didn't like it any better now than she had as a kid entering yet another home and watching the social worker and her new foster parents talking in soft voices about her.

As she had back in those days, she stood awkwardly to the side while they conversed, Rafe throwing an occasional glance at the floor of the bodega, where a bloodstained cushion and a pile of gauze were all that remained. Maybe she should at least make herself useful and clean up the mess.

She moved toward it, reaching for the nearest pile of gauze, when Rafe called out past his brothers, "Leave it. The police will want to take pictures."

Of course. How could she have been so stupid? While it wasn't a crime scene, a crime had been committed against the woman. In fact, Cassie could see a clear trail of blood droplets from where Samantha had careened into the bodega, begging for help. Some of those drops were now smeared from the feet that had tracked across them.

A knock sounded at the door. It was then that she realized someone had locked it behind her. Or maybe it automatically engaged whenever the door was closed. It had been propped open, hadn't it, when she'd arrived at the shop with Rafe?

Santi went over, twisting the key in the lock and pushing the door open. Two police officers stood outside, and she caught sight of more than one patrol car just beyond the entrance, blue lights flashing.

The brothers gave the officers a rundown of what had happened and what Samantha had said. A cup of something hot was shoved into her hands, and when she looked up, Carmelita stood in front of her. "You looked like you could use something," she murmured.

"I'm fine."

"You are almost as pale as my Rafael."

So Cassie definitely wasn't the only one who'd noticed. "Is he okay?"

"His *mami* and *papi* were killed here. I think what happened today has brought it back."

Shock rippled up her spine and pooled at the base of her skull. He'd said his parents had died, but he'd said nothing about them being murdered. "He said he lost them."

"Yes, to some *hijo de perra* with a gun, who wished to take what they had worked so hard for."

The woman probably shouldn't be telling her any of this—Cassie was a complete stranger. But Carmelita seemed like more than just an employee. She seemed like family. She had called Rafe "hers."

"Rafe said you weren't related to them."

"To the Valentinos? Not by blood, no. But this is a close community. *La familia.* We take care of each other."

"I see."

Insiders and outsiders. And Cassie was definitely one of the latter.

Rafe had told her the bare minimum about his life and family, and after doing so had wanted her to keep what she'd learned to herself.

He'd told her nothing of consequence. Yet, in a very few sentences, this woman had revealed a whole lot of heartache.

Rafe appeared beside her. "The police want to hear your version of the events."

"Okay."

Perhaps Rafe suspected his manager was sharing secrets, or maybe the officers really did want to take her statement, but he deftly separated them, murmuring something to Carmelita who replied with a "Pfffft" and a toss of her head. Here was one woman who wasn't intimidated by him. Or by any of the brothers, for that matter. She should take a page out of Carmelita's book.

Because Rafe put her on edge in a way no man ever had, not even her fiancé. Darrin had brought out softer feelings, like caring and trust—for all the good that had done. But Rafe... Maybe it was the Latino blood flowing through his veins. It brought out fiery emotions and hidden passion.

As it probably would in anyone who came across him.

When she finished speaking with the police, Rafe offered to drive her home, even before the scene had been cleaned up. "Please let me help."

"No need. My brothers and I will handle it."

The image of the group of them huddled together came back to mind.

Well? What of it? She wasn't related to any of these people. In fact, the only reason she and Rafe had been together at all today had been because of their jobs.

And that stupid time they'd spent at Mad Ron's.

He'd said it was an anniversary, hadn't he? An anniversary of what?

She glanced at the blood on the floor, the breath hissing from her lungs. Surely not. But from the way those whiskey glasses had been lined up, it very well could have been. Hadn't she thought that he was a man in just as much pain as she was?

If what she suspected was true, he'd been a man in much more pain than she could ever imagine. Because he hadn't been scorned by a fiancée or cheated on or any of those other things that people suffered on a regular basis. His experience had been so much worse.

His parents had been killed in this very bodega.

And Rafe had had to stand there while they'd been working on Samantha. And from the look on his face, he'd been wondering if the past was coming back to pay him and his brothers a visit. A visit that might end up being just as deadly as what he'd faced all those years ago.

CHAPTER FOUR

"YOU SHOULD HAVE seen his face, Bonnie. It was eerie."

"That's horrible. I can't imagine going through something like that."

"Me either." Cassie stabbed a bite of broccoli from her plate, suddenly wishing she'd canceled their dinner date.

Chez Paris was one of her favorite restaurants. It was expensive, but since she didn't eat out all the time, she felt like she could splurge periodically. At least that's what she'd told herself when she'd left the house that morning. It all seemed so different now.

But it was their "thing." She and Bonnie had taken to coming here once a month when they'd started working at the hospital. And now that Cassie was footloose and fancy-free…

Yes, and she was determined to keep it that way. Footloose. Free. No more impulsive moves on her part.

Like picking up men in bars?

That didn't count. She'd been angry and hurt and had wanted to get back at her ex in any way she could, even though Darrin would never know about what she'd done.

"So you said this CDC guy has a few cute brothers?"

The interest in her friend's voice made her roll her eyes. "Forget it. I already told you, they're taken. Or some of them are. It's hard to remember whose name is whose, much less their marital statuses."

"Are they all as gorgeous as the one who came to the hospital?"

Yes, but this was a line of conversation she didn't want to follow. She tried to shrug it off.

"They come from the same family, so of course there's a resemblance."

"So, like I said, they're all gorgeous."

They were all attractive, but Cassie had to admit she'd only had eyes for Rafe. Maybe that was because she'd spent the night with him.

And, boy, what a night that had been.

She was smart enough to know that sex often brought with it some level of emotional connection, but she'd be a fool if she let herself think there could be anything more to it than that. Hadn't she already gone down that path once before?

Her date with Darrin Myers had turned into two. They'd slept together and the relationship had taken off from there. If she looked back on it, she could see that they'd let things get out of control, the whirlwind romance turning into an engagement within three months.

It had lasted all of a year.

But they'd seemed so compatible, and she'd been happy to be swept off her feet—wanted—for once in her life. Happy to finally feel a sense of belonging.

Still, Cassie had always been one to take things slow and easy, never rushing into anything.

Like having sex with a complete stranger?

Evidently, since that's what she'd done with Rafe.

"Don't get any ideas, Bonnie. I don't know any of them."

"Not even that Rafe guy? Seems to me that you know him quite well. At least from what you told me."

"It was one night, and it was a huge mistake. I'm not involved with him, and I'm not planning on getting involved with him, so you can find yourself another wingman."

"Rats. A girl can hope." She took a bite of her chicken and swallowed. "Any word on the stabbing victim?"

"Not yet. Rafe said he'd let me know if he heard anything from Alejandro—one of the brothers. He rode in the ambulance with the woman—Samantha."

"It's hard to believe people can do such horrible things. Was she trying to kill Samantha? Or just steal the baby?" Bonnie paused. "I guess it doesn't really matter what the motive was. It would have been a death sentence for the poor woman either way. It's just plain evil."

"The police think the fiancé's ex-girlfriend was trying to get back at Samantha for 'stealing her boyfriend.'"

As soon as the words had left her mouth Cassie's muscles tensed. Hadn't she tried to do the same thing by sleeping with Rafe? Get back at her ex?

But she hadn't harmed anyone in the process, not Darrin and not Rafe. If she'd hurt anyone, it had been herself.

"I hope she makes it," Bonnie said.

"Me too. I'll send Rafe a text tomorrow and see if he knows anything."

"You could always send it now. Surely he's heard something?"

Cassie glanced down at her watch. Eight o'clock. Still early by Miami standards. When he'd dropped her off at home that afternoon, she'd decided she was going to steer clear of Rafe Valentino and his brothers if at all possible.

But she did want to know how Samantha and her baby were doing. And if the woman—Bridget?—who'd attacked her had been apprehended. "Okay, but I'm not going to send him ten messages just to satisfy your curiosity."

"This would make how many messages?"

"One, but you know what I mean." Bonnie knew how to get her to crack. She pulled her phone from her purse and clicked the button to open the window, only to stop in shock. "Well, that's strange."

"What is?" Bonnie asked.

She had a missed call, and a voice message. From Rafe.

"Mmm...maybe this is something." She hit the icon and put the phone to her ear.

A rich, familiar baritone filled her ear. "Listen, Cassie, my boss and a few folks from Washington are flying in tomorrow to look at the cases you sent me. Is there any way you can come to the office and fill them in in person? Let me know what your schedule looks like, and I'll try to work around whatever you can give us. There will be a couple of doctors from other hospitals joining us as well. I'll be waiting for your call."

That last line made her swallow, which was ridiculous. She listened for more, but that was the end of the message.

Don't get excited, Cass. He only wants you to call because he has some folks coming in.

Then it hit her. Yikes. Folks from Washington wanted to talk to her?

"Anything?" Bonnie's voice brought her back from her stupor.

"No."

Her friend's brows went up. "A whole lot of something went across your face as you listened to that message, so don't give me that."

"I don't mean 'no' about that. It just wasn't about Samantha or what happened today at the bodega. It seems some bigwigs are coming to town tomorrow and want to interview me about the Zika scare."

"So it's a scare now?"

"Wouldn't it be a scare if *you* were pregnant?"

"Yes, of course. But I don't have any prospects, so that's not even on my horizon."

"Ditto." Thank heavens she didn't have to worry about that.

She and Darrin had decided to wait on having children.

You dodged a bullet there, that's for sure.

"So what time is this meeting?"

"He didn't say. Just said they'd try to work around my schedule."

For the first time, Bonnie didn't try to turn her words around into a joke. Her brows came together. "Are we seriously looking at an epidemic in the making?"

Were they? Cassie couldn't remember the last time some fast-moving disease had landed on their shores from other parts of the world. And she hoped this turned out to be a big lot of nothing. But from the sound of Rafe's message, people in very high places were beginning to get worried.

"I don't know, Bonnie," she said. "But I sure hope not."

Rafe met Cassie at the front door of his office building, walking her through the sign-in process and making sure she went through the metal detectors without incident. She was the last of the medical staff in the Miami area to be called in for an interview, her schedule not having allowed her to make it before five o'clock.

They were waved through the last of the checkpoints, where Cassie's purse was searched and her cell phone was tagged and placed in a small locker for her to retrieve when she left. His bosses were taking no chances, and he couldn't blame them. This was a touchy situation that could easily turn into mass panic if not handled with care. The news was already having a field day reporting on the gruesome possibilities of the virus traveling from place to place through mosquitoes and sexual contact. It had the makings of a catastrophe. There were already warnings about pregnant women traveling to places where Zika was known to be. Would Miami soon be one of those places? The tourist industry was a huge source of income for many folks. To have that suddenly shut down...

Rafe didn't even want to think about it.

Nor should he. This was about saving lives. He hoped everyone could keep their focus on that and leave the financial implications for another day.

As they walked down the hallway, Cassie touched his arm. "Is there any word at all on Samantha?"

His mind went blank for a few seconds. "Samantha?"

"The woman who was attacked yesterday."

The blood on the floor of the bodega flooded his memory. He'd flashbacked to his parents' deaths eighteen years ago. The floor had been slick with blood on that day too. And his father's labored breathing as he'd lain on the floor…his mother's lack of response. She'd been dead at the scene. And his brother…

Don't think about it.

"Alejandro said she's holding her own."

"The baby?"

"They delivered him by C-section. He's alive. The knife pierced his arm, but it didn't damage any tendons or ligaments. A couple of sutures and he was good to go. He'll have no lasting damage." Unlike Samantha, who would probably be haunted by what had happened for the rest of her life. "They also found her fiancé. He's devastated. Said he never dreamed his ex would do anything like this."

Of course, Rafe had never imagined he'd have to make the decisions required of him after the shooting. But he had. And then he'd had to stand beside a bed knowing how things were going to end. He never wanted to do that again…never wanted to be responsible for deciding if someone's life support should be cut off, his heart placed into someone else's body.

If he hadn't done it, though, Alejandro would be dead too.

Dante had told him time and time again that he'd made the right decision. Papi had been brain-dead. The last-ditch effort to save his life through surgery had failed and caused a massive brain bleed.

But seeing his father in that bed had been surreal.

His familiar face had been infused with color, even though it had been the machines that had kept his blood oxygenated, that had kept his heart alive. Despite the grim prognosis, it had been hard for his teenaged mind to comprehend that his dad would never again open his eyes or recognize the faces of his sons.

Signing the paper that would turn off the ventilator had been pure torture. He hadn't wanted to do it. But to linger over the decision meant that Alejandro—whose heart had been hit by one of the bullets and damaged beyond repair—would die. There'd been no time to grieve. No time to process what was happening.

No time to say goodbye.

And so Rafe had given the okay, kissing his father's cool cheek one last time and smoothing his graying locks back from his forehead. Then it was over. His dad had been wheeled away and prepped for a surgery he would never return from. There was no going back. Or reconnecting machines. They'd buried their father next to their mother and then stood vigil over Alejandro's bed until he'd woken up. Not long afterward, Santi had disappeared, unable to deal with the tragic events. It had taken Carmelita to bring them all back together again.

If he lost one of them…

This was why Rafe didn't do relationships. His brothers were his blood, he was stuck with them. But unlike Alejandro and Santi, Rafe could choose not to link his life to someone else's. That way, there were never any difficult goodbyes. Just a few superficial friends and temporary lovers. Nothing painful. Nothing permanent.

"I'm glad she's okay."

He blinked back to the present to find Cassie watching him with curious eyes. He could just imagine what she'd been thinking.

"They're still looking for her attacker, but at least they know the woman's name and where she lives."

When they arrived at the conference room, Rafe paused. "Do you want coffee or anything before we go in?"

Her teeth came down and caught her lip. "What should I expect in there?"

"There will be a lot of detailed questions. Most on the panel are medical experts, so don't feel like you need to translate things into layman's terms, they'll want specifics. They've already interviewed a few other doctors from your hospital."

Cassie frowned. "I knew there would be other doctors, but I guess I assumed they were all from different hospitals. Why didn't they just bring everyone from Seaside in as a group and interview us together? It would have saved them some time."

"You're all on different schedules. And each person's perceptions are different. They didn't want you comparing stories and changing details."

"Wow. It sounds more like an interrogation than a fact-finding trip."

He reached over to give her hand a reassuring squeeze and found her palm clammy. His throat tightened. It took some guts to come down here not knowing what to expect. "It might seem that way, but they want to figure this thing out as much as you do. As much as I or anyone else does. Don't let them intimidate you. Just answer their questions to the best of your ability. I'll be right there with you."

"Thank you." She took a deep breath, and her eyes found his. "I mean that."

"Ready?"

"As ready as I'll ever be."

Fifteen minutes later, Cassie accepted the panel's offer of a break and a glass of water. The questioning had been grueling, and she was again thankful that the hospital had gotten permission from the patients' families, otherwise she would have been hobbled by HIPPA laws. As it was, the experts had asked whether they had found bites or rashes on any of the new mothers, and exactly what each woman had said about being ill.

It brought back a lot of the heartache each had faced as they'd given birth to their babies. Two more hospitals had recently come forward with cases that seemed to fit the parameters. The panel could have withheld that information, but she was glad that they were willing to share bits and pieces to help her with future cases.

Then she was back at it. When the last question had been presented, the experts turned it around, giving Cassie an opportunity to quiz them on the subject.

"How close are we to a vaccine being developed?"

The person she had already guessed was the head of the panel slid his glasses further down his nose and peered at her over the top of them. "Not as close as we'd like to be, I'm afraid."

She imagined this question had been asked by every person who'd sat in this conference room today. Including Rafe?

Throughout the questioning he had sat beside her rather than going to join his colleagues behind the table. She very much appreciated his support. He hadn't touched her or tried to speak over her or given her hints about what to say. He'd just quietly stayed in his seat as she'd spoken, his pencil and paper untouched in front of him. Maybe he had eidetic memory or something.

Or maybe he just wanted to help.

Isn't that what he'd said everyone in that room wanted to do?

It made her feel a little less alone. And maybe even a little less like an outsider. She appreciated that more than anything.

Then it was over and the panel stood, the men and women coming over to her little table to shake her hand and thank her for coming. She expressed her own gratitude for being able to share what she'd observed at Seaside. They all expressed hope that a solution could be found so that lives could be saved and fetal health restored.

Once outside the room, Rafe sucked down a breath. "Sorry that was so tough."

"It wasn't as bad as it could have been. I get where they're coming from, and you're right. We all need to work together to find a way to beat this."

"Thanks for seeing it that way. Not everyone was that gracious."

She stopped and looked up at him. "People from my hospital?"

"No, not yours, but County and one of the others seemed to be more worried about covering their collective asses than anything else. They clamped down on giving us any usable information."

"Wow. Did they come of their own volition?"

"Yes, that was the strange part. They could have

refused to come. Instead, they each showed up with a lawyer in tow."

That was strange. Especially for a public hospital that had to watch every penny they spent.

"Would the CDC have subpoenaed them if they'd decided not to attend?" And if she had turned down their invitation, would they have handed her a piece of paper with a judge's signature and forced her to appear?

"If it was deemed necessary for public safety then, yes, they would have. I've seen it happen."

"I guess it's a good thing I didn't say no, then." She was a little irritated that Rafe hadn't told her straight out that it was more a command performance than a simple request.

"Hey." He stopped her, touching her with a finger beneath her chin, tilting her head until her eyes met his. "We're not enemies, Cass. We're on the same team. I promise."

Were they? Didn't teammates know a little about each other? She and Rafe might not be enemies but they were still basically strangers. Just like the foster homes she'd gone through. She'd barely scratched the surface in getting to know one set of parents before another set had taken over.

Even Cassie could see the similarities between those temporary relationships and this one. Rafe was just one more person in a long line of acquaintances—people who came into her life for a season and then walked right back out of it.

She sighed. "I know. It's just been a trying few weeks. Your friends can be pretty intense."

"Yes, they can. And you did a great job handling it…and them. They were impressed by you."

"How do you know that?"

"I could tell by the way they were taking notes." He started walking again.

"And yet you didn't write down a single word."

"I didn't need to."

"Really? Why not?"

"They were the same questions I asked you a few days ago. I have my notes from back then. It was one of the reasons they wanted to speak to you. You were quicker about suspecting Zika than some of the other medical personnel in the area."

"Renato's neurologist thought the same thing I did."

"Yes. And he told us that you were the one that brought the possibility to his attention."

Dr. Blackman had said that? Her face heated. She'd just done what anyone would have under the circumstances. Renato's mom had practically shouted the word Zika when Cassie had said the baby's head was a little smaller than it should be.

It didn't really matter who had done what, as long as someone figured out a cure, or at least a way to prevent this from happening to other babies...to other mothers.

"As long as it helps create awareness, that's all that counts."

"I agree." He glanced at her with a frown. "I'm sorry it took so long. Have you eaten dinner yet? You look exhausted."

Maybe because she was. It had been a long day. "No, I came straight from the hospital." She glanced at her watch, surprised to find it was almost nine at night and her last meal had been at...

She'd had some yogurt for breakfast, but nothing since then. Great. Her cupboard was pretty much bare too, and the thought of having to stop to grab something on her way home wasn't appealing at all.

"I have some leftover Chinese food in my fridge. We can heat it up, if you don't mind me firing up my computer to transcribe some of my notes."

"I thought you didn't take any notes."

"I took plenty. Just not during your time with the panel."

Okay, so Chinese sounded really wonderful, and it meant her fried brain didn't have to make any decisions about food. Her stomach gave a convincing twinge, reminding her that she had to eat to live.

"Food—any kind of food—sounds wonderful, but it's really late. Are you sure you want company?" If he thought she was exhausted, then he must be equally so, if he'd put in as many hours today as she suspected he had.

"It'll keep me from falling face-first onto my computer keyboard."

Cassie grinned. "No one has ever invited me to dinner for that reason. Should I be flattered or insulted?"

"Definitely flattered."

Her insides warmed as she followed him out the front door, his murmured goodbyes to the people manning the front desk rumbling across her skin. He seemed like a hard ass in some ways, and yet he was courteous enough to acknowledge other people. He could have just strode out the door without a backward glance. Even at Seaside, she'd seen some of her colleagues walk past the nurses' stations without a word of greeting. She knew doctors were busy, but so was everyone at the hospital. It still irritated her from time to time.

As she settled into the leather seat of his car, and he adjusted the radio to play some soft jazz, her body relaxed for the first time in several hours. Leaning her head against the seat, she let the music wash over her, the saxophone soothing her jangled nerves. "I like your choice in music."

"I'm glad. We have about a fifteen-minute drive to my condo, if you want to close your eyes."

"I'm fine." Even as she said it, she knew that wasn't exactly true. It had been a crazy hectic day. One that wasn't done yet. No matter how hard she fought it, her lids began to creep downward. Soon she was cocooned in darkness. As the mournful strains of the next song came through the speakers, they coaxed her further and further down a well-traveled road. A drowsy, comforting road that welcomed her home.

CHAPTER FIVE

WHY HAD HE brought Cassie here?

Because she'd helped by coming to his office today and answering the panel's questions? So had a lot of other doctors and he'd invited none of them home.

But Cassie had looked so tired, and she obviously hadn't eaten anything all day.

That should have been his cue to take her to her own house, not bring her to his.

She'd made it pretty plain, though, that she had no interest in relationships, so they were on the same page. Maybe that's why he'd felt safe about it.

Parked in the reserved spot at his condo in Coral Gables, he sat there for a moment or two and watched her sleep. With her head tipped toward him, lips barely parted, and dark lashes casting shadows on her cheeks, he suddenly realized that there was nothing safe about being here with her.

He'd gotten the same gut-kicking sensation the morning after they'd made love, when he'd woken up and realized he'd spent the entire night with her. And then, instead of hauling his butt out of the place, he'd stood over her for what had seemed like hours.

And now she was here. At his home.

Not smart, Rafe. Except his condo was fairly close to his office building, at least by Miami standards. Located five miles off the Dolphin Expressway, the complex lay halfway between his parents' bodega in Little Heliconia and the Miami branch of the Florida Health Department. He was the CDC's liaison there, since they didn't have an actual branch in Miami. It was easier to pay Rafe a consulting fee than to fly someone down to Dade County every time someone called in with a problem.

Except Zika had brought the actual bigwigs zipping their way.

Taking a deep breath, he clicked open his car-door locks, trying to decide whether to carry Cassie up to his unit and let her nap on his couch or to wake her up.

Safer to wake her up. Carrying an unconscious woman up the stairs might get him a second look, even though he'd lived in the building for a few years. His government job didn't pay a whole lot, but with the bodega and his freelance work it allowed him to live in a nice area of the city.

He touched her cheek. Silky smooth, the contact sent a shard of some shadowy emotion spearing through him. "Cass? We're here."

Sleepy eyes fluttered open, the blue irises dark and slumberous.

This is what she would have looked like if he'd woken her up that morning in the hotel.

He was glad he was getting to see it. He'd imagined it in his head over and over. But the reality was far beyond anything his mind could have dreamed up.

"Hey, sleepyhead. Do you think you can make it up the stairs?" His building was right in front of them. A few blocks over from what was fondly known among the locals as Miracle Mile, Rafe found he could walk to get whatever he needed. His second-floor condo unit boasted a nice view of the pool and manicured grounds. It was all he could have asked for, and more.

She sat up with a suddenness that dislodged his fingers from her skin, blinking a few times. "I am so sorry. I don't know why I did that."

"It's been a stressful few days." At least it had been for him. He'd had meetings and conference calls ever since Cassie had called the office a week ago. And he didn't expect things to let up anytime soon. Zika was the last thing anyone wanted to see get a foothold in Miami. And although a quicker test for the disease was just becoming available, that would do little to stop a mass panic, if many more cases came to light.

"I guess so." She shook her head as if trying to rid it of any cobwebs. "I think the more likely answer is that I didn't meet my caffeine quota for the day."

He smiled. "That's one thing I can help with. Have you ever had a Heliconian espresso?"

"No."

"Well, get ready, then. You're in for a treat."

Fifteen minutes later, Rafe balanced two demitasse cups and the silver pourer containing the coffee on a tray and carried them into the living room, where Cassie waited. Fido—his traitorous cat—lay curled on her lap looking more than pleased with himself.

I bet you are, buddy. Don't get used to it. She's not staying.

He'd never had a woman up to his place. And now he knew why. It was far easier to invite someone in than to escort them back out. Even harder was saying a permanent goodbye to someone who was lodged in your heart.

The muscles in his jaw tightened. He was thinking about his father. Not Cassie.

"I can't believe you named your cat Fido." The tips of her fingers tickled over the Maine Coon's long gray fur.

Yep, definitely a traitor.

"I can't believe you called yourself Bonnie."

Her lips gave a wry twist. "Okay, I guess I deserved that. I had no idea who you were. You could have been crazy."

Any laughter disappeared. "And you thought a simple name change would protect you?"

"Not crazy like in a slasher movie. I just didn't want things to…" She shrugged. "I had just gotten out of a difficult situation. One I wasn't looking to repeat."

"You thought I might blow up your cell phone asking for a second date?"

Her face turned pink. "Something like that. I needn't have worried, since you were gone when I woke up."

That was more about self-preservation than anything. But he wasn't going to tell her that.

He poured coffee into one of the small white cups and handed it to her.

She accepted the espresso, glancing at the tray and then at him. "No sugar bowl?"

"No need. Sugar is part of the brewing process. At least in Heliconian coffee. It's similar to making Cuban coffee."

She waited until he came and sat beside her before lifting the hot beverage to her lips.

Dark and sweet, with a thin layer of foam on top,

he loved his homeland's java. He could barely drink what he thought of as *agua sucia*—that light-colored concoction most Americans seemed to favor.

Her brows went up, and she took another sip. "It's delicious. Did you use an espresso maker?"

"No. Most people in my homeland couldn't afford something so elaborate. We make it on the stovetop, and then whip a small amount of the brewed coffee with sugar until it's thick. You probably won't want to drink several in a row." He smiled. "You did say you wanted caffeine, didn't you? Well this has it in droves."

"I'll remember to go easy."

Like she had on the whiskey at the bar? The face she'd made as that first swallow had gone down had been something to see. She'd changed her mind about having another. Not so with his coffee. She seemed to be savoring it, her eyes half closing as she swallowed, tongue darting out to catch the taste of it on her lips. A rush of warmth spurted through his gut that had nothing to do with the scalding beverage and everything to do with the woman herself.

Time to get up.

He slugged down the rest of his drink. "I'll just go and get the leftovers heated."

"I can help." She glanced down. "If you'll tell me how to remove Fido without hurting his feelings."

He wasn't sure he wanted her following him into the kitchen. Not with the way his thoughts were beginning to stray from food to other things. But unless he wanted to explain why, he didn't have much of a choice.

"He's a pretty easygoing fellow." He set his cup back on the tray and reached for his cat, unable to stop a smile as the animal flopped onto his back on Cassie's lap. "I think he likes you."

Who could blame him? Rafe was beginning to like her too. Maybe a little bit too much.

"He's cute. You don't seem like a cat kind of guy, though."

"Really?" He finally succeeded in lifting a very limp Fido and setting him on the couch beside Cassie's hip, her light scent drifting his way as he did. He had to admit, he was in no hurry to move away. "And what kind of guy do I seem like?"

"I don't know." She studied him for a few seconds. "I see you more with some kind of muscular dog. Maybe one of those illegal breeds."

"Illegal? Like pit bulls?" The breed had been shunned in Dade County for years because of the proliferation of dog-fighting rings. "I don't know whether to be flattered or insulted. I would never be involved in dog fighting. Or harming any animal. I actually disagree with the ban."

She looked surprised. "I know you wouldn't. I'm sure you'd give any pet a great home, judging from Fido here."

"He knows he has it made." He leaned down to give the cat a scratch behind his ear. "I'm on the go a lot, so it didn't feel right having a dog. Fido is pretty self-sufficient and I can always ask one of my brothers to come over and feed him, when I can't be here."

"That makes sense."

Fido didn't need to be walked daily, and shutting a dog up in the condo while he worked long hours, even in a unit as large as his, didn't seem fair. His cat, on the other hand, had made the perfect companion ever since he'd brought him home from the animal shelter three years ago.

"Well, he's a very lucky cat." Cassie stood, picking up the tray and waiting for him to lead the way into the kitchen.

Halfway there, she paused. "What's that?"

"Hmm?" He glanced at her to see her attention focused on the silver stuff sack that contained his flying gear. He'd left it propped against the wall after a flight he'd taken yesterday afternoon. "It's my paraglider."

Her eyes widened. "You actually do that?"

"Yes, why?"

"Well, because it involves being in the air."

He smiled. "That's the idea." There was more than one way to escape the past. Paragliding just happened to be the method he'd chosen. "You don't like heights?"

"No. Nothing higher than standing on a counter to reach into a cabinet, actually."

He wouldn't have guessed that of her. "Remind me not to invite you to go with me, then."

And why in the world had he even said that? Paragliding was the last thing he wanted to do with her. He moved into the kitchen to shut down that line of thought.

"Just set the tray on the counter, if you don't mind."

She did as he asked, walking around the kitchen, still exploring, her fingers sliding across various surfaces. He tried not to remember about how luscious those hands had felt as they'd trailed across his skin. He failed miserably.

This was exactly the reason he liked paragliding.

Turning away, he yanked open the door of the refrigerator, searching for the take-out boxes, when her voice came from behind him. "I was wondering what happened to that."

"What happened to what?" He leaned back to see what she was talking about and froze.

Dangling from her fingers was the black elastic circle Cassie had worn in her hair a little over a month ago. He'd set it in an empty fruit bowl in his kitchen and had meant to throw it away. Instead, he found himself toying with it whenever he was in here.

Forcing himself to continue retrieving the food containers, he said, "It ended up mixed with my stuff when I left the hotel." It wasn't quite a lie. The hair tie had gotten mixed with his things, but only because he had been the one to drop it into his pocket. He still didn't understand exactly why he'd done it.

He closed the refrigerator door with his hip and set everything down, only then realizing she was still staring at the tie, her face tense. "Cass?"

She looked like she was battling with something she wanted to tell him. Finally, she forced the words out. "My fiancé cheated on me the night I went to the bar. Or at least that was the night I actually caught him. I had suspected for a while, but he denied it, so I thought…" Her eyes came up. "He had me believing I was being paranoid. Or crazy. But I wasn't. God…I wasn't at all. How could he do something like that?"

A tight ache settled in Rafe's chest. Going over to her, he took the tie from her fingers and set it back on the counter. Then he wrapped his arms around her. "I don't know. But from the sound of it, you're better off without him."

"I know, but it doesn't make it any easier."

He cupped her face in his hands, thumbs sweeping

over the delicate bones of her cheeks. He repeated the words, emphasizing them. "You're better off without him. Say it."

"It's hard to—"

"I want you to repeat after me." He gazed down at her, the tightness in his chest morphing into something softer. "I, Cassandra Larrobee, deserve better than to be with a man who makes me feel anything less than amazing."

Her teeth toyed with her bottom lip, and she stood there for a long minute, then her arms went around his neck and she stretched up to drop a light kiss on his cheek. "Thank you."

He should have moved back then, while he still could. He waited for that sense of self-preservation to kick in and carry him to safety, but there was nothing. The switch wasn't working.

Instead, one arm slid across her back, drawing her near. Then a very different kind of switch turned on, and his mouth came down on hers. The intimate touch scorched across his senses instantly, like lightning hitting a pile of brush.

As if caught in the same fiery trap, Cassie made no attempt to move away. Instead she edged closer, her arms tightening further.

The hell with the food. He had all he needed right here. Maybe it was the heat from the coffee and the jolt of caffeine talking, but suddenly every nerve ending he possessed came alive in a rush, each clamoring for what this woman had to offer.

Pressing her against the refrigerator, Rafe's fingers went to the back of her head, where another hair tie bound the silky strands into a single thick rope. He wound it around his hand, fingers closing over it like a lifeline.

Maybe it was.

All he knew was that finding her back in his arms fueled a craving that had been growing despite all of his efforts to squash it. Or at least do some serious damage control.

Screw it. He was going to let it happen.

Maybe they'd met again for this very reason. He hadn't quite gotten her out of his system a month ago, so it was up to him to really do it right this time.

With that in mind, he lifted her onto the countertop, scattering the take-out containers he'd put there moments earlier. She gasped as their mouths lurched apart, and she gave a shaky laugh. "I thought you brought me here to eat."

"Well, this wasn't exactly the kind of eating I had in mind..." he planted a kiss on her throat "...but what's in front of me looks pretty damn delicious."

"Oh!" Her legs parted, her feet hooking around his knees. "What if I need more seasoning?"

"What better seasoning than coffee?" He leaned in for another kiss. "I can taste it on you. Best pot I ever made."

In truth, the woman didn't need anything. She was hot and sweet and spicy all at once, and he couldn't seem to get enough. Of any of it.

He reached for her hair elastic, tugging it free and then tossing it on the counter behind him. "And that makes two."

She leaned back and shook her hair out. "You're lucky I have more of those at home."

"Oh, I'm definitely lucky." He said it against her ear, reveling in the way she shivered against him.

Her fingers slid away from his neck and went to the buttons on his shirt, undoing the first three. Then the three after that. Soon she had his shirt tails pulled free from the slacks he'd worn to the meeting this afternoon, her palms grazing the planes of his chest.

A certain part of him stiffened painfully, wanting to forget about the appetizers and get right to the main course.

But he also wanted this to last.

His mouth skimmed her collarbone then followed the rounded neckline of her top. No buttons on this one. Zipper? He checked the back and found just silky fabric and the thin line of a bra strap beneath his touch. So it had to just…

He grasped the material at her waist and bunched it in his hands and then lifted it up and over her head. It went without a fight.

There was indeed a bra underneath it, but it was lacy, almost sheer—playing peek-a-boo with his senses. He closed the gap between them, his erection finding the hard edge of the countertop when what it really wanted was warm, soft flesh.

As if sensing his need, Cassie wiggled forward.

Yes.

He cupped her hips and dragged her to the very precipice, until he could feel her tight against him.

When she reached behind her, he thought she was trying to steady herself. A second later, her bra straps fell from her shoulders and slid down her arms, proving him wrong. She tossed the garment onto the linoleum floor.

"Holy hell, woman."

Made up of gentle curves, creamy skin and high, tight nipples, her breasts were perfect. Just like he remembered. And when his hands covered them, she arched into him with a gasp. "I thought it might be hard to eat if the wrapper was still on."

"It is. Very hard." She might be talking about her bra, but he was talking about something entirely different. He showed her with a single tilt of his hips.

"Rafe…"

His lips went to her breast, nibbling his way toward the center and then suckling hard on what he found there.

"Ahhh…" She gripped the back of his head, pressing him against her, asking for more.

Damn, she was everything a man could want.

He continued feasting, holding her with his teeth while his tongue scrubbed over her flesh.

She moaned. "I don't want to wait."

Her hands went to the front of her slacks, undoing the button and jerking down the zipper. He backed up a step to watch, loving the way her hips jiggled as she shimmied her way out of the garment, taking her panties off with them. Then she leaned back and spread her legs.

He swallowed.

She was more gorgeous than anything he'd ever seen, and he wanted her.

Was going to have her now.

He tugged his wallet free of his pocket, going through the same motions he'd done the last time they'd been together. Except this time Cassie held her hand out for it. "Let me."

"I don't think—"

"Trust me." She smiled. "I promise to be gentle."

His smile was a little tighter than hers had been. "I'd rather you weren't. I can handle a little bit of rough-housing."

"Oh, yeah? Then take off your clothes."

She said it in a tone of bravado, but her cheeks went a delicious pink. She was experimenting. Trying to act uninhibited when she was anything but.

He liked it. Liked believing she'd never spoken to another man the way she was speaking him right now.

And he wanted it to continue. Even if that meant stripping down in front of her. Because if she could dish it out, he could certainly take it.

"You've got it, babe."

Taking a step back, he made short work of his trousers, keeping his eyes on her as he kicked them off his legs. As he did the same with his briefs, Cassie flipped open his wallet and found the little compartment where he kept his condoms.

Someone had paid attention the last time they'd been together.

He moved forward again when she tried to rip open one of the packets with her teeth and failed.

"Not as easy as it looks, is it?"

"The execution doesn't matter as long as it happens."

"Honey, from where I stand, execution is everything." He took the packet from her and opened it without hesitation. "Especially when all I want to do is take you in a rush."

She sat up straight, reaching for him. Finding him. "Then do it. Take me."

With that, she trailed her fingernails lightly down his length, forcing a deep groan from him that was totally involuntary. When she started to repeat the act, he grabbed her hand and held it.

"Not so fast, *mi querida*." He dropped the condom on her palm. "We need this."

Cassie placed the latex shield on the head of his erection and slowly rolled it over him.

Once he was covered, he took her hands and set them on the counter. "Now we're going to play a game."

"A g-game?"

She didn't sound quite as brave as she had a moment earlier when she'd been ordering him to take his clothes off. And although his body wanted to comply and charge right through to completion, his mind wasn't quite ready to hand over the wheel. Not just yet.

"Yes. An eating game, since you reminded me that's what I brought you here for." He went to the refrigerator and rummaged through it for anything that might work. "I'm going to turn my back and count to fifty, and you're going to lay out a taste test. On your body. I have to guess what the treat is, and which body part it's painted on."

She moistened her lips, and he halfway thought she might chicken out on him. He set the items he'd found next to her hip, hoping for the best but ready to swallow his disappointment if she balked. "Are we on?"

Up went her chin. "Turn around and start counting."

So he did, trying to keep his body in line as he imagined her smearing chocolate sauce, and whipped cream and cherries over that luscious skin.

Something behind him hissed to life. Hell, the whipped topping. He lost count for a second or two, his palms moistening as he tried to find his place. Maybe he'd be the one who chickened out.

He hit fifty.

"Ready?" His voice wasn't quite as steady as it had been.

"More than ready. You can turn around, but keep your eyes closed."

He did as she asked. A second later, her hands were on his and she guided him toward her. His length slid over the same counter it had earlier and found her. Lost her. She must have moved slightly backward.

"Uh-uh-uh. Not yet." He could almost hear her smile. "Since there are five food groups, I've made five taste zones. I'll guide you to each of them, and you'll...taste."

Her breath hitched for a second. "And then you'll have to guess what it is, and *where* it is. Number one..."

Something softly touched his lips. He immediately opened and drew the object inside, sucking lightly. Dark. Sweet.

He knew what it was and where it was, but he didn't want to let go to guess. Cassie obliged, pushing what had to be her finger further into his mouth, mimicking what he was dying to do to her. The third thrust found him opening his mouth and letting her go.

"Chocolate." He reached up and found her wrist, bringing it slowly forward so he could kiss her digit. "On your finger."

"You're good at this," she whispered.

"Not bad for my first time playing."

There was silence for a second or two, then she cupped his cheeks and guided his head forward and down. "Here."

He opened his mouth, his tongue sliding to find the object. Oh, he knew what this was…and where. But he could have a little fun while he was at it. He wrapped his lips around her and lost himself in the taste and texture of her breast. Without coming up, he murmured against the puckered flesh. "Whipped cream…and nipple. Both are delicious, by the way."

He moved in for another taste, and Cassie moaned, her hands going to his butt and pulling him against her, spreading further. Waiting.

No. He had to finish the game. Releasing her, he tried to control the jolt of disappointment his body sent him. "Next."

Her belly button had strawberry sauce drizzled in it. He swirled his tongue inside to capture the very last drop, hoping against hope she was going to keep him moving in this direction.

"Rafe…" The way she said his name sent a shudder rippling across his midsection. He didn't need any guiding this time, easily finding her knees with his palms and pushing them apart.

He went down on her, the fragrance of marshmallows melding with her own personal scent.

It was intoxicating. Addictive. And he wanted it. Now.

Using tiny strokes of his tongue, he explored and lingered. Her hands moved to hold him in place, but she needn't have bothered. He had no intention of going anywhere. Yet.

She didn't ask him to name the flavor, and he didn't offer up his guess, allowing himself to glory in the soft heat beneath his mouth instead. Cassie's hips set up a rhythm, nudging that tiny part against him, her breathing becoming ragged. Needy.

"Oh, Rafe, I'm going to…"

He opened his eyes to find her head thrown back, eyes closed, her nipples hard and pink as she continued to push against him. And then he felt it. Every muscle in her body tightened, drawing up, going rigid.

She cried out, and up Rafe came, finding her immediately and thrusting home in a rush. He rode out her orgasm and then allowed his own to race in and capture him, grabbing her to him as the massive wave crashed over him and into her. Again and again he rode that wave until there was nothing left but shaking legs and a woman who had brought him to a point he'd never reached before. Ever.

He caught his breath and looked for his sanity, then pressed his forehead to hers. "That was…"

"I know."

A few seconds of silence while he tried to steady his muscles.

"Who knew good nutrition could be so much fun."

Her words were so unexpected that he laughed, the sound half-choked as he looked at her.

She giggled too, her fingers sliding up and down his back.

He kissed her nose. "I don't know about good nutrition, but it was definitely *good*. So the fourth flavor was marshmallow cream." He searched her body for the missing treat. "What was number five?"

"I think you forfeited the game with that premature—"

"Watch it." But he smiled as he said it. Because they

both knew it hadn't been premature. It had been unstoppable. "But seriously. Number five?"

He couldn't imagine anything sexier than what she'd just put him through.

"Are you sure you can handle it?"

A glimmer of doubt raised its head. Could he?

"Try me."

With him still deep inside her, Cassie reached over and picked up a bottle of maraschino cherries and popped open the lid. She reached in and grabbed a stem, slowly pulling the little red fruit from the jar. Opening her mouth, she dangled the cherry over it, her tongue darting out and licking the bottom of it with a soft moan.

Something down below tightened—started to come to life again. He gulped. "Do it."

"Are you sure?"

"Very."

With that, Cassie wrapped her lips around the red fruit and plucked the stem from it before it disappeared in her mouth.

Rafe needed no further invitation. He moved in and took her mouth in a feverish kiss that had them both back at the starting line. A place he could get used to far too easily.

A place he needed to find his way home from. Before it was too late.

CHAPTER SIX

IT HAD BEEN a week since the last Zika meeting at his office. And a week since she and Rafe had made love in his apartment.

She'd been feeling out of sorts on and off for the last three weeks. Today it had progressed to downright nausea that sent her scrambling for the bathroom just off her bedroom. She had no idea why she felt so awful. Maybe her cycle was getting ready to...

Her thoughts barreled past that reason before screeching to an abrupt halt and backing up a few paces. Then a few more.

Her period.

When was the last time she'd had one?

When? Oh, God... *When*?

A series of dates raced through her head, and she discarded some and tried to think her way through others. She'd never been all that regular, but surely she should have had one by now?

But the stress...

She *had* been under a lot of stress with the worries about the Zika virus, and with having to work so closely with Rafe, but surely that wouldn't throw her system off so completely?

But what else could it be?

She flushed her bathroom toilet, even though she hadn't thrown anything up, and went over to the sink, splashing her face with water.

She and Darrin had always used protection. Always. And if she was pregnant with that man's child, she was going to have a nervous breakdown. Even the thought of telling him had her kneeling beside the toilet all over again.

They had been so careful.

But things happened. How many times in her career had she heard that such and such a baby had been the result of an accident?

Far too many.

Climbing back to her feet, she placed a hand on her belly and glanced down at it. "Hello. Anyone in there?"

She immediately felt ridiculous. And terrified.

It couldn't be Darrin's.

Back at the sink she stared at her reflection, then her eyes widened, her hand going to cover her mouth.

"Oh, no. It can't be." But the way her tummy flipped up and over made her wonder. She and Rafe had done things that she and Darrin had never even dreamed of...and they'd remained connected a whole lot longer before separating than she and her ex had.

She blinked, leaning closer, realizing her cheeks had hollowed out a little over the past month. From the Zika scare? Even as she thought it, the tummy that had been flipping around sank like a rock.

Zika. Could she have somehow contracted the illness? Was that why she'd been feeling so weak and ill?

Ha! It hadn't stopped her from making love with Rafe in that hotel room, and then back at his condo.

They'd had sex multiple times on both occasions. That brought her right back to the first option: she could be pregnant.

She didn't even want to think about the implications.

You don't even know if it's a possibility, Cassie. Let's not get ahead of ourselves.

"Okay, so what do we do?" She rolled her eyes and took her hand off her belly. "'We' can start by not using a plural pronoun. It's still only one of you until proven otherwise."

But…a baby! She didn't know the first thing about raising a child.

Are you sure? You already know what not *to do from your own childhood. They need love. Compassion. Discipline. And most of all the kind of permanent home you didn't have.*

Her jaw firmed with resolve. First she needed to know one way or the other.

She'd go to the grocery store tomorrow and buy a pregnancy test. Not at a nearby store, but one where no one would know who she was. Maybe she'd head up I-75 and venture into Broward County. Wearing sunglasses. And a wig.

"You're being ridiculous, Cassie."

But a little voice inside her whispered that she wasn't being ridiculous. She was being smart.

And Zika?

Her mouth went dry all over again.

Which would be better? Being pregnant? Or having Zika?

Better? Now, there was a word. She couldn't imagine anything worse, actually.

Unless…

She ran for the basin all over again, nausea gripping her stomach in an iron fist that refused to let go.

There was something worse. Far worse than having one of those two options become a reality.

What if she were pregnant *and* had Zika?

She sank onto the floor, the cold tile surface giving her a jolt of reality.

What was she going to do?

What else could she do? She was going buy a pregnancy test. And to pray with all she had that the result was negative.

The buzzer on his desk sounded. "Rafe?"

Carla from the reception desk. She and Stephanie—the other administrative assistant—fielded visitors and calls, funneling the legitimate ones through and deftly dealing with the not so kosher ones.

"Yep." He pulled up the latest articles on Zika. Sometimes the press was one step ahead of them, so it paid to take a look at what they'd discovered.

"Someone is here to see you."

He frowned. "Okay. Can you give me an idea who it is?"

"Cassandra Larrobee? I had her take a seat and told her I would call back to see if you were available." He could practically hear the young woman's smile over the phone. "So are you? Inquiring minds want to know."

He ignored the word play, knowing well enough how quickly things could spiral out of control.

Like inviting Cassie to his condo a week ago and then licking strawberry sauce off her body?

What the hell had he been thinking?

He hadn't. And the results had been…

Dammit!

This was the reason he never invited women to come to his place.

It was time to put this runaway train back on its tracks and send it on its way.

He had no idea why Cassie was here, but it was his chance to cool things down between them. If that was even possible.

"You can send her in. Thanks."

A minute or two later, there was a quiet knock at the door. "Come in."

She pushed through the door, and Rafe came out of his chair. Cassie's face was pale and drawn, with red blotchy areas under her eyes and across her nose. She was carrying a manila envelope in her hand.

He ushered her to one of the two metal seats. "What's wrong?"

"I wasn't sure I should come."

Her face wasn't the only alarming thing about the neonatologist. Her voice had a shaky quality he didn't like. He perched on the edge of his desk, foreboding taking hold of him. Was she here to ask why he hadn't contacted her in the last week? He should have, if only to clarify that their night together had changed nothing between them.

Oh, really?

He sucked down a quick breath, not giving that question time to sink in. Instead, he asked the obvious question. "Is everything okay?"

She didn't answer for a second, then her lips twisted and she toyed with the edge of the envelope. "No, it's not. I have something to show you."

"About the cases?"

"I don't think so. At least, I hope not. I'll know soon enough."

He had no idea what she was talking about. "You'll know what soon enough?"

"There's no easy way to say this. And I'm only here because I think you have a...a right..." Her voice faded to nothingness.

A weird pounding began at the base of his skull and traveled quickly toward the front of his head. He stood. "Is what you need to show me in there?"

"Yes."

He held his hand out, opening and closing his fingers a time or two to indicate she should pass him the envelope, even though the last thing he wanted to do was look inside.

Instead, she just sat there, the item still resting in her lap.

Irritation replaced concern. "What's this about, Cassie?"

She took a deep breath. "Just so you know, I did not do this on purpose."

Short of injecting a bunch of her patients with a fatal disease, he couldn't imagine what she could have done that was so terrible.

"Did you hurt someone?"

"I don't know. Not yet."

Okay, he'd had enough. He reached down and took the envelope from her, ignoring her squeak of protest. "Is this confidential information?"

"Yes, yes, it is. You can't tell anyone."

"I don't want you to violate HIPPA laws, Cassie, so

unless you're allowed to share whatever this is with me, then—"

"I'm pregnant."

His mind had already raced ahead to dire imaginings about contagious diseases, so he had to backtrack through several thousand megabytes of information before the words made sense. "You're...*what*?"

Maybe he hadn't heard her correctly.

"Look inside." She nodded at the envelope.

Suddenly, Rafe didn't want anything to do with the item in his hands. If he could have, he would have tossed it back at her with a dismissive laugh...and better yet, tell Carla to send her on her way before she could say anything that would crack his orderly little world more than it already was.

What else could he do, though? Call her a liar? Refuse to look inside the envelope?

Exactly how many times had they had sex? A lot. He couldn't even set a number to it.

Hell, he was in big trouble.

He lifted the flap on the envelope and let the item slide out of it. A plastic stick. A pregnancy test. He didn't need to look at the indicator to guess what the result was. The pressure in his head built to dangerous levels.

"Mierda. Santa Madre de Dios," he whispered. More graphic swearwords rolled past in his head without needing to be vocalized.

No wonder she looked ill. He was feeling a little queasy himself. "Are you sure?"

Her hand touched his. "Yes. I'm sorry, Rafe. I was just as horrified."

A spot of hope flared inside of him. She'd just

broken off a relationship before they were together. Maybe…

"Is it mine?"

As soon as the words left his mouth he knew they were the wrong ones to say. He waited for her to stand to her feet and slap him across the face.

She didn't, but she did take her hand off his. "I'm not positive but, yes, I think so. It could have only been my ex or…"

Or him. "Have you told him?"

"Yes. I called him this morning."

It stung that she'd called him first, although he had no idea why. He should feel let off the hook, but there was some other emotion in the spot where relief should be sitting.

"What was his reaction?"

Rafe already had a good idea. He had seen it in her face when she'd come into the bar a month ago. Had figured out the truth about her reason for leaving her ex long before she'd actually told him.

"He said it doesn't matter. He doesn't think it's his and wants nothing to do with it." She paused and blew out a careful breath, her eyes filling with tears.

He lowered himself into the chair next to hers and wrapped his arm around her shoulders. "Hell, I'm sorry, Cass. What a rotten thing for him to say."

Rafe wasn't sure he was handling this much better than the ex had, though. Man… He'd never wanted to be a father. Or a husband. Or anything else that required a commitment of more than a few hours once a year.

It was easier that way. No hard goodbyes. He'd already lost his mother and father, and very nearly lost a brother. That was enough for a lifetime.

And yet hadn't he already played a dangerous game by inviting Cassie into his home and getting a little too close?

She was pregnant. His brain swirled as he tried to find a way through all the chaos clogging his insides and couldn't seem to find an exit.

Cassie scrubbed a palm across her eyes, leaning into his touch. "It doesn't matter. Anyway, I didn't come here to talk about him. I came to ask a question."

He tensed, his insides turning to ice. He couldn't marry her, if that's what she was thinking. Or was she going to ask him to set up a college fund? Take a paternity test? Go on father/son camping trips? Hell, he didn't want to have to do any of those things. With a mouth that had gone completely dry, he asked, "What's the question?"

"I want your opinion on the Zika virus. I know you've been investigating it, and so…" She ended the words on a shrug.

Zika? What did that have to do with anything? "I don't understand."

"I'm trying to get a handle on what I'm facing. Whether or not there's a possibility that I could have it."

Realization dawned, and his dry mouth suddenly flooded with saliva. She was pregnant. If she had Zika… His head refused to cooperate. "I don't think so, unless you've exchanged fluids or…"

She nodded as if knowing what he thinking. "My ex has admitted to having…" there was a long pause "…several partners over the last couple of months. But that wasn't what I was thinking. I just meant in general.

Is there any chance I could have contracted it? From a mosquito or a patient?"

"It's possible. But not likely, given what we know. Most of the people who contracted it got it from somewhere else. There's a new test that's just been rolled out, though."

"I know, and I plan on taking it. But I thought I should warn you as well."

"Of what?"

"We both know it can be sexually transmitted. I got pregnant, so either a condom failed or we weren't careful enough." She paused. "You should probably be tested for the virus as well."

What the hell?

She'd just handed him an atomic bomb when she'd told him she was pregnant, and she was worried about him? His gut tightened painfully, as did the arm he still had draped over her shoulder.

"I'll be fine." Even as he said the words he wondered if they were true. And that thought had nothing to do with Zika.

"I'm so sorry, Rafe." She twisted to look up at him. "Like I said, I have no intention of doing anything that would affect your life."

She wasn't alone in this. If this baby was indeed his, then he'd done far more to affect her life than she'd done to affect his. No matter how or why, he'd had a part in this.

Well, hell. He wished he could say her pregnancy was impossible, but he couldn't. He'd broken rules he'd never broken before with Cassie, and he had to take responsibility for that.

He swallowed hard. "We used protection, but I

didn't always withdraw as quickly as I should have. I'm the one who should be sorry. How can I make this right?"

"You can't." Her eyes shifted away from his before coming back. "I mean, I don't expect you to do anything. It's no one's fault."

He clenched his jaw, his system threatening to shut down completely. "What do you want to do?"

"I don't know. I want to see what the Zika test says first."

The thought of her terminating a perfectly healthy fetus made his insides twist even further. But he had no right to tell her what to do. He wouldn't…*couldn't* make that kind of decision for her. Or anyone. Not after his father. He took his arm from around her, putting subtle space between them.

"If you decide to continue with the pregnancy, the current Zika recommendation is to have two ultrasounds at different times."

"Continue?" She blinked, her chin firming. "I want to keep this baby, if at all possible. I'm not making any more impulsive decisions."

Impulsive. Like sleeping with him on the heels of her fiancé's betrayal? Like him picking up women at a bar year after year to forget about his father's death?

Rafe didn't like to think of his actions causing another person harm. Or creating an unplanned pregnancy.

"How long have you known?"

"My periods have never been regular, so it only crossed my mind when I got nauseous yesterday."

The enormity of it hit him. He may have unknowingly fathered a child. Hell. She wasn't the only one who felt nauseous. He forced himself to touch her hand again, when all he wanted to do was get up and walk out of the building. "Are you okay?"

"Not really." She sucked in a breath and blew it back out. "Are you?"

"This wasn't really what I expected to hear when I came to work today."

"I was hoping I was wrong about the whole thing."

"But you weren't. I'll take a paternity test if you want. And help financially, of course, if the baby is mine."

She frowned at him, before standing to her feet. "No need. I'm quite capable of raising a child on my own. Women do it all the time."

And just like that Rafe was left feeling impotent, like nothing he said or did would change the outcome. Like his father's massive brain bleed when he'd been left with very little in the way of brain activity, just the systems that operated his heart, but as far as higher thinking? All gone. In medical terms, his father had been brain dead. And there had been nothing anyone could do to change that.

He stood as well. "Women might do this alone all the time, but you don't have to. I'm willing to help. Want to help."

As long as she didn't expect to get married.

Her eyes came up and met his. "Why would you want to? Wouldn't it be easier just to walk away and pretend this never happened?"

Before he could answer, she got a funny look on her face, her hand going to her stomach. "Trashcan. Quick."

He'd barely comprehended what the words meant

when Cassie took matters into her own hands, rushing behind his desk, picking up the stainless-steel bin and promptly throwing up into it.

"I'm so sorry." Cassie was pretty sure that was the fifth time she'd said those words as Rafe had knelt beside her, rubbing her back as she'd thrown up again and again until there was nothing left in her stomach.

His touch was been oddly comforting, and it was scary and thrilling all at the same time. If her engagement had gone the way it was supposed to, it might have been Darrin helping her as she lost everything she'd eaten this morning.

Except she couldn't picture her ex getting anywhere near her at a time like this.

You're just being all sour grapes because of what he did.

No. Cassie was pretty sure she wasn't. She'd loved Darrin.

Or had she?

"No need to be sorry."

"I'll clean your trashcan." The thought made her stomach heave all over again.

"I'll take care of it." Rafe left the room again, and she thought he had gone to find one of the janitorial staff to come and deal with it. Raw humiliation crawled up her throat. The fewer people who knew she was pregnant, the better. At least until she'd gotten over the shock of it herself.

She would have to tell Bonnie.

And her parents.

Scratch her parents. She hadn't even told them about her breakup yet. Besides, they would be all excited about becoming grandparents, and if there was a chance this baby could be affected by Zika, it was better that she kept the news to herself for a little while. Her vision suddenly went blurry as she tried to block out that picture.

She sank back into her chair, the trashcan still between her feet, just in case.

Rafe came back into the room with a wad of wet paper towels. "I don't have a sofa, or I'd have you lie down. But maybe if you put these on your forehead, it'll help ease the nausea."

He pressed the cold cloths to her head, and Cassie closed her eyes with a moan. He was right. It felt heavenly. Lying down sounded even more so. The last thing she wanted to do was to have to drive back home. "Do you mind if I lie on the floor for a minute or two?"

"That bad, huh?"

"I'm hoping the worst is over."

He helped her onto the carpet and draped the paper towels over her forehead, while he left the room with the trashcan.

She didn't mean for him to have to clean up her mess and yet she'd just handed him a whole pile of it, and none of it was in that trashcan.

That hadn't been her intention in coming here, though. She'd wanted to alert him of the risks. She believed in full disclosure.

Her lips twisted. Throwing up in front of him might have been carrying that motto a little too far.

She pulled the hair tie from the back of her head to make it more comfortable. Then she closed her eyes and relished the cool cloth and the temporary relief from the bout of nausea. Finally. At least for now.

A minute or two later Rafe was back. He held up the can with a questioning look.

"I think I'm okay. Thank you. I'll get up in just a minute."

"Take your time. When you're ready, I'll take you home."

She laid a hand on the cloth on her head. "My car is here."

"Let me worry about your vehicle. I want to make sure you get home safely."

Up went her brows. "I made it here, didn't I?"

"Maybe, but it's been touch and go ever since you arrived. I'd rather you not put anyone else at risk."

Like the baby? No, of course not. He was talking about other drivers.

He squatted down beside her. "You need to take the rest of the day off."

"It's already my day off, thank goodness." Which was why she'd chosen today to do this. Not because she'd just wanted to get it over with.

Which she had.

He glanced at his watch. "It's almost time for me to get off as well."

Thirty minutes later they'd made it to her apartment without any other 'incident,' as she was now referring to it. When she tried to climb out of the car, she swayed a time or two. And then Rafe was there beside her, swinging her into his arms and carrying her up the stairs. Then they were through the door and Rafe was slamming it shut behind him.

CHAPTER SEVEN

HE SLID OFF the sofa with a groan. This was quite a change from the last two times he'd spent the night with her. But he'd been so shocked by her appearance at his office that he hadn't wanted to leave her alone, even though it meant that he was forced to relive every word that had passed between them.

Cassie was pregnant.

With his child, more than likely.

Dragging a hand through his hair, he wondered if he should just slide out of the door and leave or whether he should check on her. But when he stretched his back—several vertebrae popping in protest—he saw a note on the coffee table beside him with something green underneath it. A smile came to his face when he lifted it and saw the words, "Taxi fare... Oh, wait, wrong occasion. This is to help get my car back to my house. Oh, and there are towels in the bathroom if you want to shower. And thanks. For everything."

Rafe stuck his hand in his pocket, and his smile widened. Another hair tie. The one he'd picked up from the floor of his office. How many did this make? Three? Maybe she should save her money to buy a few more packages if she went through them this fast.

A buzzing sound came from the dining-room table. Making his way over to it, he saw that it wasn't his phone, it was Cassie's.

The name "Darrin" appeared, along with an image of a large—and some might say good-looking—man. The picture was in the shape of a heart. That wiped the smile right off his face. It had to be her ex.

Calling about her pregnancy? Hadn't Cassie said the man didn't want anything to do with it? Had he changed his mind? Or did he just want to drive his point home all over again?

Rafe's fingers curled into his palms.

But was he any better? He'd offered her financial help, but nothing more.

Which meant Cassie was basically facing this all by herself.

Not quite. He was here, wasn't he?

Didn't that make him better than Cassie's ex?

Not really. She'd been in no condition to drive herself home.

The phone stopped ringing, probably putting the caller through to voice mail. Would she call the jerk back?

None of his business.

Going into the bathroom, he found the towels Cassie had talked about. He also noticed there was a door on the other side of the space leading...

To Cassie's bedroom.

Where she was sleeping.

He looked away, switching on the shower and dialing the temperature a little cooler than he might normally have liked before he stepped inside the enclosure. Letting the lukewarm water sluice down his body, he quickly showered, his nose picking up the slight floral scent of her soap. The thought of wearing it on his own body…

A telltale pulsing at a point in his lower half told him he should not be sending thoughts in this direction. Especially now.

But it seemed that every image in his brain right now was centered on that one area of his body. Time to put a stop to it.

He switched off the water just as he heard the door on the other side of the room open.

He hadn't locked it!

Grabbing a towel, he hurriedly wrapped it around his waist. Cassie appeared, wearing a short, silky nightgown. She was yawning and rubbing at her eyes. When she looked up, her gaze slammed against his and she drew in a breath.

"Rafe! Sorry." She backed up a pace, reaching for the doorknob behind her. "I forgot you were here."

"It's okay. I'm done." His glance slid down her body. "How are you feeling this morning? Any better?"

"Much, thank you." The door behind her opened as she found the knob. "I'll just let you get dressed before I…"

Before she went to the bathroom? Before she brushed her teeth? Before she trapped her hair in another black hair tie?

It didn't matter. What did matter was that he get out of here as quickly as possible. *Before* she decided to return her ex's phone call. Because that was one conversation he definitely didn't want to stick around for.

Cassie lay on the table, waiting for Dr. Raven Davi to come in and tell her this was all some big mistake.

She wasn't pregnant. Wasn't carrying a load of nerves over the Zika virus.

Darrin had left her a message asking her to call him. She couldn't imagine why. They'd already made their feelings quite clear to each other.

Besides, he was the reason she was lying on this table right now. If he hadn't cheated on her, they would still be engaged.

But would she have been happy being married to him in the long run?

Bonnie touched her shoulder. "You okay?"

She'd told her best friend the news that morning and Bonnie's eyes had glittered with unshed tears. They had joked their way through a lot of different scenarios, but none like this one. For once there'd been no barbed comments. No snappy rejoinders. No laughter. Bonnie was the one constant in her life. The one person besides her parents that she knew would be there for her no matter what. If things went okay, she was going to ask her friend to be her birth coach.

"Ugh, I don't know. At least I don't feel sick today."

"Are you positive you're pregnant?"

"Eight home pregnancy tests are telling me I am."

Bonnie scooted her chair around until she was sitting near the head of the bed. "It has to be that new man in your life. He's got a lot of testosterone. I can tell."

And the laughter was back. "Bonnie!"

She might be right about the testosterone part, but she was wrong about him being in her life. He wasn't. He'd merely wandered across her path on his way to...

Well, wherever he was going.

"He was just a one-night stand, Bonn."

"Really? I seem to remember your telling me there was a second night."

"Okay, so two. But neither of them meant a thing."

Her friend's brows went up. "This from someone who is monogamous about everything, right down to her brand of toothpaste and ordering fettuccine Alfredo from the pasta joint down the street?"

"Yeah? Well, maybe that all changed when my fiancé decided he didn't like the monogamous life. I can see his point. There's something heady about a secret fling."

"Oh, so we've moved from one-night stand into secret fling territory, have we?"

"What else would you call it?"

"I'm not sure. Maybe you're falling in love with Rafe. That's a thing, isn't it? Falling in love with someone on the rebound."

"I'm not falling in love. With anyone." That was a thought that didn't even bear exploring. What a disaster that would be. To fall in love with someone she barely knew.

Cassie tended toward being cautious. And Rafe was the antithesis of caution. He was dangerous to the max. To her psyche…and to her body, as evidenced by how easily she'd gotten pregnant, even using protection.

Bonnie held her hands up. "Okay, but if you wind up married to the dude someday, I am so going to sing about it at the wedding." She then put on her best country twang and belted out a few lines about finding love with a heartbreaker.

"Enough!" But at least her friend had her laughing again. "You are never to sing that song around me again. Ever."

Maybe because it hit a little too close to home right now. Rafe couldn't be the one. Could he? The tender way he'd helped her when she'd gotten sick had made tears come to her eyes. And then driving her home... spending the night on her sofa. She swallowed. Hormones. They could make you feel things that weren't really there. Or were they?

All he'd offered, though, was financial help. Not to be involved in the baby's life.

Was that what she wanted? For him to be involved? No. Not unless he could make it permanent. The last thing she wanted was for some father figure to flit in and out of her child's life. She was going to give this baby what she hadn't had as a child. Security. Love. And a permanent home. If she had to go it alone to make sure that happened, she would.

Dr. Davi swept into the room, shaking her hand. "Did I just hear someone singing?"

"No." Bonnie and Cassie said the word at the same time, and then dissolved into giggles.

"Okay, then." The OB/GYN sat on the rolling stool, pulling it closer to the bed. "Tell me what's going on, Cassie."

A long-time colleague, Dr. Davi was someone she trusted to keep her secret. And she'd asked Bonnie to be with her during the ultrasound so that the doctor didn't need to call in an obstetrical nurse. The fewer people involved in this, the better. At least until she had a handle on what was going on.

"As you know, the urine sample showed elevated HGH."

In other words, she was pregnant. She could have

told her that. "I expected that. What I'm really looking for is a time frame."

If the doctor was shocked, she didn't show it, although her glance went to her hand. Her ring was long
gone, even though she'd never officially announced the
end of her engagement to anyone other than Bonnie
and now Rafe. It was too humiliating. Especially the
reasons for the failure of the relationship.

"Do you have any idea how far along you are?"

"A little, but my periods have always been erratic.
It could be as recent as two weeks."

"I see. We're not going to see much on the ultrasound if it's only two."

She sighed. "I know."

Dr. Davi stood, "Well, let's get to it. We'll do a
trans-vaginal scan, since we can get a better picture."

"There's another thing." Cassie swallowed. "I
haven't been feeling well for the last several weeks. I
thought it was the flu but…"

"You think now it's the pregnancy." The doctor
stood and went over to the counter where Bonnie had
already set up the instruments.

"I'm hoping that's what it was."

She glanced quickly back at her. "I got the impression that you weren't exactly expecting this pregnancy."

Realizing she'd gotten the wrong idea, she shook
her head. "I wasn't. But with the Zika scare going
around…"

This time Dr. Davi frowned. "You think you've been
exposed?"

"I don't know."

The doctor came back over and sat down. "You need
to fill me in on exactly why you think this."

Trying to relay a shortened version of the events leading up to now did no good. Dr. Davi kept taking her back through the story, asking a thousand different questions.

When she'd finished, the OB/GYN said, "You have some of the symptoms, but not all of them. I understand your concerns, though. I'd be worried too. I think everyone who works in the health care sector needs to be aware of the risks. And with the patients we've had recently, I can see why it's a scary prospect to be pregnant right now." She scribbled something in Cassie's chart. "We'll do some tests and see if you show antibodies. Sometimes it'll show up like a reaction to Dengue or something similar."

Cassie knew all of this, but she was glad the obstetrician didn't just wave away her concerns. She was going to take them seriously.

Just like Cassie was.

"Thank you," she said.

Bonnie squeezed her shoulder. "Let me help the doctor finish getting the ultrasound machine ready and then I'll come back to watch with you."

She hadn't told Rafe she was getting the sonogram today. And since she hadn't called Darrin back, Bonnie—and now Dr. Davi—were the only ones who knew she was doing this. And Cassie meant to keep it that way. At least until she had some answers.

Once the ultrasound was pulled over to where everyone could see the images, Dr. Davi helped her put her feet in the stirrups and readied the probe.

Soon, pictures of her insides came into focus. The doctor checked her ovaries and then shifted to find her uterus. Pushing some buttons on the machine, she then searched the area for evidence of her pregnancy. Within seconds, they had their answer.

"There. You can see the placenta, and…" She bent closer to the screen and then changed the position of the transponder, the images whirling past.

Cassie's mouth went dry, her heart beginning to race. "What's wrong?"

Then the gestational sac came into view, and a tiny flicker of movement. A heartbeat!

"I don't quite know how to tell you this." Dr. Davi shifted the probe again and the sac appeared again.

Was she trying to get a better view? Were her trained eyes seeing some horrible defect that Cassie couldn't make out? "You don't know how to tell me what?"

She muttered something Cassie couldn't make out about "cooperating." "I'm trying to get them into the same frame."

Bonnie, who was beside her, caught something she didn't. "Did you say *them*?"

Just then Dr. Davi smiled and the screen came back into focus, revealing two black circles. "Yes. Them."

Two gestational sacs. Two tiny embryos. Twins.

Good heavens. Black spots appeared before her eyes. "Are you sure?"

"See for yourself." The doctor was marking things on the ultrasound with little Xs and then typed the letters A by one and B by the other. "They aren't sharing a sac, but as you know that doesn't necessarily mean they're fraternal. The embryo could have split in two after being fertilized, each forming its own sac."

She understood the words, but her brain was still

fixated on the fact that there were two embryos. And two chances for something to go wrong.

What was she going to tell Rafe?

Wait. "So if you can see both of them, then that means I'm further along than just a couple of weeks." She felt a moment of fear they could be Darrin's.

"Yes. I would put you at seven weeks, possibly eight, but no more."

The black spots grew. Seven or eight weeks would mean they were definitely Rafe's babies.

Her breathing stopped for several seconds. She didn't want to be pregnant at all. But if she was, why was she suddenly glad it was from a certain one-night stand that had turned into two?

Because the less contact she had with her cheating ex, the better. Hadn't she learned during her childhood that nothing in life was permanent? Darrin had certainly validated that belief and stamped it with a big fat T for true.

One thing she did know, however, was that her babies were not going to grow up believing that. And if it took shutting their father—Rafe—out of their lives completely in order to do that, then she would. No matter how much it might hurt to do so.

Rafe shifted for the thousandth time as he sat in the waiting area where he'd been directed by one of the nurses. Perfect. His appearance at the hospital had come at just the wrong time. He'd been worried about Cassie ever since he'd crashed on her sofa two days ago. But when he'd finally given in and come over on his way home from work, his lanyard had been spotted by a roving reporter there to interview the hospital administrator about the Zika virus. The reporter's "Are you with the health department?" had taken him by surprise, so he'd answered in the affirmative.

The next thing he knew, she'd been throwing questions at him right and left about this hospital and others in the area. His repeated "No comment" had been brusque, hoping to stop her in her tracks. Unfortunately, it also made him appear as guilty as sin, like he was hiding something. And he was. His reasons for coming to the hospital, which were purely personal.

All he needed was for his superiors to see the news footage and start asking some pointed questions about how he'd handled the reporter.

Handled? He'd been trying to save his ass. And Cassie's. He'd done a pretty poor job of doing either.

Just then, he caught sight of that very woman coming down the hallway, her ear glued to her cell phone. From the look on her face, it was not a happy conversation.

Getting to his feet, he couldn't hear what Cassie was saying, but he didn't like the way she clenched the phone. Her eyes widened as she spotted him. For a second she looked like she might head in the other direction. But then she stopped.

Suddenly her brows came together. "I already told you. You are *not* the father, and *no one* is going to support these...*this* baby except for me. Now, please don't call me again."

That had to be Darrin, and if...

Wait. Had she said 'these?'

"The day just keeps getting better." Cassie shoved the phone in her pocket. "What do *you* want?"

Holding his hands palms up, he allowed one side

of his mouth to lift. "If I say a paternity test, are you going to take a swing at me?"

"Very funny."

Well, at least she still had her sense of humor. "I'll say one thing, Cassie. You sure can pick them."

She lifted a brow and gave him a pointed stare. "Evidently I can."

This time he laughed. "Remind me never to make you angry."

"Sorry." Her shoulders sagged. "It's been a really long day, and I can't seem to catch a break."

"I can see that." He touched her arm, noticing she didn't shake him off. "I only have one question."

"Is it about the baby?"

"Yes, it is actually. I also came to check and see how you're doing. You have a lot more color today than you did the last time I saw you."

"Maybe because I was busy puking my guts out the last time you saw me. I'm learning if I down saltine crackers by the boxful, it keeps the nausea at bay. Actually, though, I feel much better today." She tightened her ponytail, and he noticed lines of exhaustion under her eyes. "Now, what's your question?"

He wasn't sure this was the time, but he had to know. Had to try to figure out how to deal with everything that had happened. "Why did you start off by saying 'these' when you were talking about your pregnancy?"

There was silence for several long seconds. Finally he tried a more direct approach. "Is there more than one fetus?"

Twins ran in his family. He was a twin. He had an aunt who'd also had two sets of twins.

He waited for Cassie's answer. When she did speak, she didn't look up at him.

"Yes. There are two."

Rafe's stomach bottomed out. "Are you sure?"

"I had an ultrasound this morning." She dropped into a nearby chair, and Rafe lowered himself into the one next to her.

"And the tech told you there were two?" Was he really hoping the ultrasound had been read incorrectly?

"It wasn't a tech. I asked one of the OB/GYNs to do the scan. I saw them with my own eyes. There are two babies."

His head was spinning so fast he had trouble finding anything to say for a few seconds. She must have sensed his confusion because she started to get up. He stopped her with a hand on her arm. "Please, wait."

When she sat back down Rafe put his elbows on his knees, his hands folded in front of him, as he tried to make sense of things. He couldn't remember being at such a loss since the time he'd sat in a waiting room very much like this one, hoping beyond hope that he'd made the right decision, and that Alejandro would survive his surgery.

"Are they okay?"

"It's hard to tell at this stage. Their hearts are both beating."

His throat tightened. His father's heart had been beating as well, only he hadn't been okay at all. And now, although that heart continued to beat, it was in Alejandro's chest. "Can they tell anything at all?"

"Not for a while. Blood tests can check for chromosomal damage, but as for Zika, the doctor is doing a test to check for antibodies."

He unclasped his hands and shifted his body to look at her. He hadn't lied when he'd said she had more color than she'd had two days ago. She was beautiful, her eyes soft with concern, maybe because she knew how conflicted he was.

But there was no way she could know that. No way she could know how painful it was to hear about beating hearts and uncertain days.

"You're sure they're mine?"

"I'm seven or eight weeks along." Her voice was quiet. "I haven't slept with my ex for probably ten or eleven weeks."

"I guess that settles it, then."

"Yes." She covered his hand with hers. "I'm so sorry, Rafe. I wish I could rewind the clock so that none of this had happened."

So that they hadn't slept together? Or so that her ex hadn't cheated?

He wasn't even sure he wanted to know the answer to that question. "We used protection." They'd already covered this territory, but he kept coming back to this one point.

"Sometimes it fails. You know that as well as I do." Her hand left his, and she stared straight ahead.

"Hey." He slipped his fingers under her chin and turned her back to face him. "I didn't mean that as an accusation. I was trying to take away some of the guilt. You didn't set out to get pregnant. Neither of us did. It could just as easily have happened with Darrin."

"How did you know his name?"

He swallowed back his guilt. He hadn't been snooping. "Your phone rang while you were asleep the other morning. I was standing near it and his name came up

on the screen. There was a heart and so I assumed…
There's no chance you'll work it out with him?"

"No. I want to put that time in my life behind me."

Would she one day say that about him? About the
time they'd spent together?

He wasn't sure why, but that thought made him un-
easy. "I want to help."

"Not necessary. Didn't you hear what I told Darrin
on the phone? I'll raise them by myself."

"Don't you think they deserve to know their father?"

She sighed and leaned back against her chair. "I just
want to make it through today, Rafe. And then tomorrow and the next day. I can't worry about what might or
might not happen seven months down the line. Besides,
if the tests come back positive for Zika antibodies…"

Her voice faded away, but he knew exactly what she
had been going to say.

If there was a possibility that the babies were exposed to the virus—one that made barely an impact on
the mother, while wreaking havoc with any baby that
might be growing in her womb—she might be faced
with yet another problem.

And just like his father's death, Rafe would be
powerless to help her.

CHAPTER EIGHT

DANTE VALENTINO CRADLED Renato in his arms as he took the baby from his mother. During the course of all the testing they'd discovered that the sagittal suture in his skull had prematurely fused. The resulting cranio-synostosis would force his head to expand along the other sutures, causing it to become narrow and elongated if not corrected.

The neurosurgeon who'd been called in to examine the baby would have to be Rafe's brother—her luck wouldn't have it any other way. The two men had the same dark hair and dark eyes, but although Rafe had said they were twins, they didn't look any more alike than Rafe's other brothers. Except they were all equally hunky.

The sight of him holding that baby made her wonder what Rafe would look like holding theirs.

Except he might never choose to do that, especially after she'd said she wanted no help. It had probably been a mistake to blurt that out, but she desperately wanted her babies to have a stable, loving environment, free of people walking in and out of their lives. But wasn't Rafe right? Didn't she have an obligation to allow him to see them?

She didn't know.

Dante stood and placed the baby on the exam table next to his mother's hip. "I've seen his chart, and I know the craniofacial surgeon has already been in to see him, but I wanted to do my own assessment."

She knew his surgery schedule over at Buena Vista Hospital was a killer, so the fact that he'd come all the way to Seaside to see Renato touched her. The brothers' parents had definitely raised the boys to be compassionate, no matter how hard they might try to hide it. Dante was as gruff as Rafe. Maybe more so, if the rumors around the hospital were to be believed. And yet he cared about Renato. Just like Rafe had seemed to do when he'd insisted on examining the baby in person.

Cassie touched the young woman's hand. "Do you have any questions for Dr. Valentino?"

The baby had progressed remarkably well, his breathing problems all but gone, and as far as developmental milestones went, so far he seemed to be hitting them all, except for his head size and the craniosynostosis. Whether that was caused by the Zika virus or was just one more incidental finding was unknown. Either way, the suture fusion would have to be corrected.

Renato's mother was ecstatic that the news wasn't worse, as she'd heard of severe cases of microcephaly in her home country from the virus. Women were afraid of getting pregnant, including the woman's sister.

"The surgery. It will fix his head size?"

Renato's mom had been fixated on that one point. Maybe she thought if his head was a normal size it would mean he would be free from any lingering problems. The truth was they might never know fully what variants had been caused by the virus and what hadn't. It would likely take years of research to determine that.

"It will allow his brain to grow and encourage his skull to grow along normal lines." Dante glanced at the mom. The answer was succinct, not withholding information but not handing out false hope either.

Like the kind she'd been dishing herself? Realistically there was less chance that she had been exposed to Zika than a lot of the women who came through Seaside. But that would change as the virus got more of a foothold in the country. There would be more Renatos, unless a way was found to fight either the virus or the mosquito vectors.

"You can do the surgery?" Renato's mom asked.

"I'll do it in conjunction with another doctor. We'll need to set a date. You'll still be in the country?"

"Yes, we live here now. I wished Renato and his brother to have what I did not."

The woman had a lot of reasons to rail against the universe for what had happened to her son, but she wasn't. She seemed grateful for everything Seaside could do for her and her baby.

Maybe Cassie should focus on the good things about her own life, rather than dwelling on the terror of the unknown. There was nothing she could do to change anything at this second in time. She could figure things out as they came at her. Not the way she normally lived life, but right now it was all she could do.

Dante looked up at her. "Seen Rafe recently?"

Even as the question registered she could feel the heat building in her face. He didn't mean anything by it. He knew that she and Rafe had seen each other because of their respective jobs, but it didn't make her any less uncomfortable. Did the brothers know she and Rafe had slept together? That she was pregnant?

The epidemiologist didn't seem like the type to kiss and tell, but his siblings and Carmelita had seemed inordinately interested in her at that meeting at the bodega. Thank heavens Cassie hadn't known she was pregnant at the time or they might have seen something in her face that gave it away.

Had Dante seen something now? Something she wasn't quite able to hide?

"We've met to discuss some of the cases, yes." That was pretty vague, wasn't it?

His brothers were eventually going to find out. Unless Rafe intended on keeping the whole thing a secret. She couldn't see him walking away from his kids, though, no matter how many times she told him she wanted to raise them on her own.

Dante made a soft sound. She had no idea if it was about Renato, or about what she'd said. And unless he told her otherwise, she was going to choose to believe it was about their patient.

The man took out his own measuring tape and wound it around the infant's skull, writing down the measurement. "He may need to wear a helmet to help shape his head for a while."

"A...what?" The woman looked confused.

Cassie drew the shape of a helmet with her hands. "It's a kind of hat that will help his head grow in the correct direction. How long will he need it?" She directed that question at Dante.

"A year or so. It's part of the baby's recovery plan. The surgery will get the process headed in the right direction, but the helmet will make sure he has the best possible outcome."

Dante held one hand on the baby's chest to keep him in place while he scribbled on the chart. The crinkle of the paper cover beneath the baby seemed inordinately loud in the room.

"I will do anything to help him. My family..." The young woman swirled her hand in the air, as if searching for the right word. "They very worried about Renato." She glanced toward the baby as if wanting him back.

Dante must have sensed it too because he laid down his pen and picked the baby up, carefully cradling him in two hands, and handed him to his mother. He glanced at Cassie. "I'll let the hospital know that he'll need to be put on the surgical schedule. Make sure she has the paperwork."

"I will." Surgeries like this one, where there was a specific window in which the repairs needed to be done, were marked on a huge calendar at the nurses' station. It not only reserved a surgical suite, it also served to make sure there weren't any gaps in treatment. Surgeons like Dante were in short supply and wait times could be long.

He rolled his tape measure and dropped it in one of his pockets. "Tell Rafe hello when you see him. And that we need to have another family meeting. Soon. I heard he's been spending quite a bit of time in the air lately." He said it with a smile, but a shiver went over Cassie.

She assumed being "in the air" meant Rafe was going up in that glorified parachute. Maybe his brothers were worried about something happening. Except it hadn't sounded like that. "I'm sure you'll see him before I do."

Brown eyes met hers, crinkling at the corners. "Oh, I doubt that. How about whoever sees him first has him get in contact with the other?"

Once again, heat flashed up her neck and oozed into her face. The last thing she wanted was for Rafe's brother to tell him she was itching to see him.

"That's not necessary. At all. I'm not in a rush to see him." She gulped as the little white lie came to her lips. "We only see each other about business anyway."

Dante reached a hand out to Renato's mother. In it was a business card. "It was nice to meet you. We're going to do everything we can to make sure Renato gets the care he needs. If you have any questions, please feel free to get in contact with me."

He was giving out his personal number? Surely not.

But hadn't Rafe given the patient's mom his private cell phone number as well? It would seem that these men really did care about making life easier for their patients.

What about for the women in their lives?

That was a question better left unasked. Two of the brothers were married. So were Dante and Rafe the last holdouts of the family?

She didn't have time to wonder for very long, though, because with a nod and a last stroke of the fuzzy hair on top of Renato's head, Dante was gone.

"Can I talk to you for a minute?" A figure separated himself from the wall of the hospital corridor.

Relief swamped Cassie's chest that it was Rafe and not Darrin. Although she really didn't expect to see her ex again, since she'd reassured him the babies weren't his. And that she didn't want any of his money. He'd seemed relieved it was over.

"Sure." She slowed so he could fall into step beside her. "I haven't had any more suspected cases of Zika this week, if that's what you're going to ask."

"It was. In part."

The "in part" made her stop to look at him. A horrible thought filtered through. Had Dante called him after he'd left the exam room and told him she was looking for him? Because that would be just too...too... mortifying.

"I talked to Dante."

Oh, hell. She was right. Her heart rate sped up to a painful rate. "I honestly didn't tell him I wanted to see you, so I don't know what he—"

"You were with Dante? When?"

Her brain screeched to a halt. "Well, not 'with' in a personal sense. We were discussing a case."

And why had she felt the need to explain any of that? If anything, it made her feel guiltier.

"Which case? He didn't say a word to me. He just said that he was going to operate on one of Seaside's suspected Zika babies and I was curious if you knew which one."

Of course that was the reason. Although why he'd come all the way down to the hospital to ask was beyond her. "A phone call wouldn't do?"

Rafe's gaze left hers for a second, wandering down the hallway before coming back. "That brings up the 'in part.'"

She knew there was something more to it than what he'd just said. "Okay."

"I was going to ask you not to say anything to my brother about your…" His fingers fluttered toward her midsection in a way that made her laugh.

"About the babies? Why would I say anything to him about that?"

"I don't know. I thought maybe you were excited and wanted to share the news."

Was she excited?

Yes. She was. More than she wanted to admit. But he had to know she wouldn't go blurting it out to everyone she came across.

"I haven't told anyone except my friend Bonnie and the obstetrician. My mom and dad don't even know yet. And I don't plan on telling them until I know for certain that everything is…"

His jaw tightened. "Until you know for certain everything is okay?"

"Yes. I don't want to worry them unnecessarily."

"How long before you tell them?"

She stopped in front of the window of the nursery where Renato's cot was, staring through it at the baby. "I'll have another ultrasound in a few weeks. Once I know the babies are developing normally, I'll tell them."

She wanted to just ignore the possibility that something could go wrong. But, of course, burying her head in the sand wasn't an option. And it wasn't in Cassie's nature to close her eyes and pretend things were fine when they weren't. She hadn't done that with her ex's cheating, and she couldn't afford to do it with the babies.

And if her Zika tests came back positive? She didn't really expect them to, but it still worried her. Maybe because the embryos she carried inside her were innocent. They'd done nothing to deserve contracting the virus.

Neither had Renato. He seemed happy enough, despite everything. He was cooing and so much less agitated than he'd been when he was born. Was he going to be able to overcome his difficulties?

Cassie hoped so.

But right now she needed to make sure Rafe knew the score. "I'm not going to show up at the bodega and announce my pregnancy to your family, Rafe, if that's what you're worried about. That is not up to me."

"Isn't it?"

Maybe he felt the same way as she did. That he didn't have a right to say anything without her permission. If that was the case, then she was grateful. "Like I told you earlier, no one knows but Bonnie and my doctor. And you. I plan on keeping it that way for a while. I'd appreciate if you did the same."

"I have no intention of telling anyone."

She should be grateful for that. Instead, a zing of pain went through her at his tone. He certainly hadn't signed up for a pregnancy when they'd had that one-night stand. But she hadn't signed up for it either. She and Darrin had been together for a year without a single pregnancy scare. And yet one night with a stranger and *bam!* she was expecting not one but two babies. It couldn't have come at a worse time.

"You are off the hook. In fact, I remember saying that once before. I don't expect—or want—anything from you."

Rafe stared at her for a minute as if she had two heads, then he reached out and grabbed her hand, tugging her into an empty exam room. He whirled around as soon as the door closed. "Do you think that's why I came here? To tell you I wanted nothing to do with the babies?"

There was a strange prickling sensation behind her eyes. "Isn't it? Maybe it's for the best anyway."

"For who? You? Or the babies?"

"I don't even know what's going on with them yet—or if they'll develop normally."

"I haven't asked outright yet, but I need to know. Are you considering terminating the pregnancy?" A muscle twitched in his cheek.

Did he want her to? Was that what his reaction was about? Hoping that he wasn't going to have to deal with her and the babies?

She owed it to him to be honest, though. "No, actually, I'm not. I want to have them."

Rafe's eyes closed for the tiniest second. "Thank God."

He wanted them? But a few seconds ago he'd been warning her about telling his family. "I don't understand."

"My brothers…" He took a step forward, threading his fingers through hers. "We've suffered a lot of loss."

"Your parents."

"Yes. It makes it hard for them—for me—to expect things to turn out well." One side of his mouth went up. "And in my line of work you expect disaster to strike at any time. Maybe that's why I went into epidemiology. So that I could make a difference…sound a warning before it's too late. Something my brothers and I were not given."

"Carmelita shared a little bit about what happened."

His smile faded, even as he sighed. "Why am I not

surprised? She's been taking care of my brothers and me…for a very long time. So she thinks she can just poke her nose in wherever she wants to."

"She loves you all. I'm sure she considers you part of her family."

His fingers tightened on hers. "We consider her a part of ours as well." His gaze slid to her midsection. "Enough about my brothers and Carmelita. So you're feeling better?"

"Yes, thank goodness."

He chuckled and tugged her in a little closer, sending a whoosh of surprise through her. "I liked the little parting gift you left me at your apartment. I guess I deserved that."

"You did. Leaving a girl money after you spend the night with her is never a good idea. I hope you didn't do that to anyone else."

"No, you were the first one. The only one."

The way he said those last three words sent a shiver through her, even as his other hand went up to her ponytail, tugging lightly on it. "I really was worried about you getting home."

"Why that time?"

That muscle went to work in his cheek again. She thought he was going to brush off her question but then he said. "Because I didn't expect to fall asleep that night."

She blinked. But they'd done it how many times? It was a bit fuzzy in her skull. She remembered a whole lot of pleasure coming one right after the other. So he didn't normally do it more than once? Or he didn't normally spend the entire night with his one-night stands?

Ha! Well, if they'd stopped at just once she probably wouldn't have gotten pregnant in the first place.

Rafe either drove his women home after he had sex with them, or they had their own car. Neither of which had been true that night.

"I guess I can forgive you, in that case."

His cheek slid against hers, the slight stubble sending a jolt of surprise through her—and leaving a tingling awareness in its wake. Heat poured into her midsection, spreading quickly. Her nipples tightened in reaction.

"You forgive me? Are you sure?" he murmured. "Don't you want to exact some type of revenge?"

"Revenge?"

She wanted to exact something, that was for sure. How could her hormones be racing a thousand miles a second when a few days ago she could barely walk without feeling like she needed to head for the nearest trashcan?

Maybe because this man was the sexiest thing she'd ever encountered. He'd been kind to her patients, and to her. But it was more than that. There was just something about him that got to her.

He'd fathered her babies. That had to be it.

Something more hovered at the edge of her thoughts, looking for a foothold. She gave her head a little shake to force it to go away. She was pregnant, and Rafe was a handsome man. Of course she was imagining things that weren't real. That couldn't be real. It was just the protective side of her looking for a caregiver for her babies.

Her babies did have a caregiver. Her. But Rafe had

offered his help as well, and right now he was standing in front of her looking like he wanted to...

Like he wanted to kiss her.

CHAPTER NINE

RAFE KNEW HE was in trouble the second she looked up at him with those big blue eyes. Actually, he'd known he was in trouble the night he'd picked her up at the bar. He just hadn't expected to ever have to face her again after that evening.

And yet here he was in an exam room, dying to kiss her.

He didn't try to fight it, just lowered his head and touched his lips to hers. Not in fiery passion, the way they'd come together on those other two occasions, but more like...

Lovers.

Maybe it was the fact that she'd said she wanted to keep his babies. Maybe it was because with her face clean-scrubbed, her hair pulled back in a ponytail, she looked open and honest. He liked that. Maybe a little too much. Whatever it was, the second his mouth covered hers, he was lost.

He gathered the length of her hair in his hand, winding it around and around, feeling her head tip back as the slack disappeared. And that low hum of need she made...

Okay, that chased the sweetness of his touch toward

something that was far less innocent. Rafe's tongue slid across the seam of her lips. She parted them just enough that he had to push forward, her mouth closing around him in a way that said his thoughts weren't the only ones veering into oncoming traffic, dodging all the things that told him to stop, but were instead plowing recklessly ahead. It was exhilarating. And terrifying.

"Cass?" He kept his mouth against hers, hoping against hope that no one was about to burst into the room. Maybe they should take this somewhere else.

"Mmm?"

"Are you still on duty?"

"Just getting off. And you?"

His body clenched at her phrasing, his hands going to her ass and tilting her into him. "Not quite yet, but my thoughts are definitely headed in that direction."

"And are you ready to? Get off?" She bit his lower lip with enough force to make him hiss in a breath.

All thoughts of going somewhere else fled as raw need hit him with a crushing force. "What do you think?"

"I think we might be able to make it work."

The words percolated through his brain. Was she talking about the two of them making a relationship work? He hadn't even thought about it, but suddenly he wondered why it would be so impossible.

She's talking about sex, you idiot. Nothing else.

But the kernel had already taken root, like an infection that invaded one cell and then moved on to another. Doing his damnedest to ignore it, he took her mouth again, forcing his mind back to what he'd started, his libido suddenly whipping into high gear, wanting her like he'd never wanted any other woman.

He braced his back against the door and reached under her scrub top, trying to find the elastic of her pants. She pushed his hands away and did it for him, shoving the stretchy waist down to her knees.

"Your zipper," she muttered, her fingers finding his button and deftly undoing it, while he was a shaking mass of nerve endings. She freed him within seconds.

Before he could even try to wonder how they were going to do this without her taking her bottoms all the way off, she turned away from him, pressing herself against his pelvis and then bending at the waist.

"Oh, hell."

There was no need for condoms, and Rafe couldn't remember the last time he'd been skin to skin with a woman. The heady scent of her arousal washed over him. It would only take a second...

Except it was true, it would only take him a second or two and he would be done. Gripping her left hip with one hand, he reached around and found her, pulled her tight against him and used his thumb to stroke and caress, wanting more than anything to be deep inside her.

And when she angled her hips and found him, he couldn't fight it any longer. He thrust deep, still very aware of the need to barricade the door behind him. He leaned over and bit her earlobe. "I'm about to let the whole world know what we're doing in here if my ass starts banging against the woodwork."

She pushed hard against him. "How about if I do the banging?"

And she did. While he continued to tease her soft

flesh, Cassie rocked her hips, taking him deep and setting up a punishing rhythm. Without being able to control the speed, he was fighting a losing battle. He gripped her hips tighter, trying to slow her just a little. Instead, her fingers slid over the ones that were working at the V of her thighs, helping him get the job done.

And that was it. He was over the top, gritting his teeth to keep from crying out just as the wet heat around him clenched tight, pulsing against him in a way that told him he wasn't the only one who'd just leapt from that particular cliff. She kept moving several times more, her fingers slowing as she continued to contract, her breathing loud and irregular.

A few seconds later she gave a pained laugh. "God. I can't believe we just did that."

He couldn't either. But he'd liked it. Liked that she'd trusted him enough to have a quickie in a hospital room. That she'd helped him fulfill the ultimate fantasy.

But not only that. She'd given him the first glimmer of hope in a world that had seemed very dark.

He loved her. And Rafe knew he would never be the same.

"You what?"

Three days later, Bonnie was in her apartment with a bag of microwave popcorn hanging loosely from one hand. Cassie took it before the woman dropped it. She leaned in closer so that Bonnie could hear her. "We had sex in an exam room."

"Why are you whispering?"

The loud words made Cassie jump. And then laugh.

"I have no idea. It was crazy and exciting. And I'm never doing it again."

"You're never having sex again?" Bonnie grabbed a bowl from a kitchen cabinet and waited while Cassie ripped into the bag of popped corn and dumped it into the container.

"You know what I mean. I'm never having sex at the hospital again."

"Not even in his car? In the parking garage?"

The fact that her brain stopped to think through the ramifications and possibilities made her blow out a breath. "I am in so much trouble."

"No. You're not. But you could have been. Taking chances is so not like you, Cass."

Her friend was right, it wasn't. It was much more like something Bonnie would have done. What had gotten into her?

Besides Rafe.

That thought made her giggle again. Wow, something was misfiring in her head.

"Are you thinking dirty thoughts?"

"I think you have passed some terrible disease my way."

Bonnie smiled. "I've heard women get horny when they're pregnant. A lot."

"I've been as sick as a dog." Except she was feeling better.

"Evidently not sick enough to stop you from *having sex in an exam room*!"

"Why are you yelling?"

"Because I'm jealous. And happy for you."

"Happy for..." She shook her head, dropping the

bowl onto the countertop. "Don't get any strange ideas. It was sex. That's it."

"And yet you made a baby. Two of them. And even after you found out about them, you're still having sex with him." Bonnie picked up the bowl and headed for the living room. "He's not running. And neither are you."

Her friend was right. She wasn't running. And she should be. So should he. They had made the ultimate mistake, and yet they'd come together again like two horny adolescents. Maybe it really was the baby hormones pushing her to do things she shouldn't.

What was Rafe's excuse?

She followed Bonnie, chewing on those words. What *was* his excuse? He'd seemed happy that she was going to keep the babies. And minutes later he'd been bending her over and...

Well, she'd technically bent herself over. But that was neither here nor there. They'd had sex. Meaningful sex. Cassie couldn't deny it. That first time she might have been able to blame Darrin's infidelity, rationalizing that it had fueled a need to get even with him. But the second and third times? No, that had been all about Rafe. And wanting him.

The thought that had been skating around the edges of her skull for the last two days finally pierced her meninges and stabbed deep into her brain.

What the hell was she thinking? She couldn't. There were too many potential landmines with that scenario. Rafe didn't do commitment—he'd as much as admitted it. He slept with a different woman at least once a year. A woman he had no intention of ever seeing again. He was not the kind of stable, permanent figure she wanted in her life. In her babies' lives.

Could she trust him to stick around for the long haul?

She didn't think so. And that was the problem. She didn't want her twins growing up the way she had, wondering if this home was going to last or if it was going to split apart at any second.

She wouldn't put them through that.

It had been fun and sexy to sleep with him, but wasn't she setting herself up for heartache by continuing down this road without asking some hard questions?

"Hey, daydreamer, did you hear me?"

"Um, no, sorry. What did you say?" She forced her mind back to Bonnie, who was already sitting on her couch, her freshly painted toenails propped on the coffee table. Bonnie had declared that they both needed a girls' night out, complete with mani-pedis, even though that was a luxury Cassie never allowed herself. Maybe she should crack open one of the beers in her refrigerator. What the hell was stopping her?

The same thing that was stopping her from hoping that what was going on between Rafe and her was something that could last.

An abundance of caution.

She was pregnant. No drinking for the next several months.

And Rafe?

She groaned out loud. She had the next few months to decide what to do about him. Or did she? Wouldn't rushing ahead with a relationship be the worst kind of mistake? The same kind of mistake she'd made with Darrin?

"Cassie! I swear. Are you thinking about doing him again or something?"

"Oh, Bonnie, I'm sorry. Say it one more time. I promise I'm listening."

Bonnie rolled her eyes. "I said do you want a horror or a comedy?"

"Can I have one of each?" Because the last two and a half months had contained elements of both. And she had no idea how to separate the two, or if she even could. All she knew was that she loved the man.

And she was terrified that she was going to pay for it in the worst possible way.

Bonnie touched her hand. "Oh, sweetie. I don't know if I should congratulate you or express my deepest sympathies."

Before she knew it, she was crying into her bowl of popcorn, looking at her freshly painted fuchsia nails and sobbing even harder. "I don't know either." She sniffed, accepting the tissue her friend handed her. "I'll let you know when I do."

Squeezing her hand and then releasing it, Bonnie picked up the movie. "I vote horror. It'll give you less time to think and more time to scream."

Cassie smiled and mopped her face before letting herself fall into the sofa cushions behind her. "Good idea. I think that's just what the doctor ordered."

"Great. Hold tight to those munchkins and get ready for the ride of your life." Her friend nudged her with her elbow. "Wait. You've already had that, haven't you?"

"Movie, Bonnie. Movie. No more cracks about my love life."

She couldn't take talking about it any more than she already had.

"Okay, but it won't be easy." She selected a movie from the choices on the screen and pressed play. "So all of the Valentino brothers are now taken, except one?"

"Bonnie…" She allowed a warning note to enter her voice, trying not to let her hopes jump too far ahead of her. Because Rafe wasn't taken. Not by a long shot.

She wasn't sure he ever wanted to be. But she needed to find out.

So for now she would just watch movie characters slice and dice each other, and try very hard not to think about the slicing and dicing she might soon have to do. She would face that bridge when and if she came to it. Even if she didn't dare cross over it.

From what she'd seen, Rafe didn't believe in forever any more than she did. And she couldn't let her babies pay the price for her poor choices. She knew from her own childhood what was at stake, and she wasn't willing to play games with their future.

In the end, she would sacrifice anything and everything for her twins, even the chance to have a relationship with their father. Because that's all it was right now: a chance, an uncertainty that might lead nowhere. Unless Rafe could promise her more than that, it wasn't a chance she was willing to take.

Rafe leaned forward to kiss Cassie on the cheek, only to have her duck away from his touch.

Not the reaction he'd expected.

Stuck in meetings for the last two days, he'd been looking forward to seeing her. To discussing what had been percolating in his brain during their time apart. That he would like to see where things between them might lead.

When he'd spoken with her on the phone this morning, she'd seemed just as eager to meet him. She'd even set the place of the meeting: the parking lot of the hospital. He figured they would go to a special restaurant…and then? Who knew?

He leaned a hip against the side of her car, studying her face. "Is everything okay? The babies?"

"Yes, they're fine, as far as I know."

"Good." A few muscles relaxed. Maybe he was just imagining things. "I hope you're hungry. I made reservations for us at Casa Lucia. I thought we could go back to my place afterwards."

Her eyes widened. "Oh, I'm sorry, Rafe. I wish you would have asked."

His muscles went back on high alert, a strange foreboding growing in the pit of his stomach. "You already have plans for this evening?"

"No, I don't have plans. As for meeting here, I just…" She stared at the keys in her hand, as if already planning her escape. "Things have happened really fast between us, but I think it's time to stop and take a breath. To slow things down a little."

"Slow things down?" Things were a hell of a lot slower now than they'd been the night they'd met. And with her pregnancy he'd suddenly felt a sense of urgency—the need to hurry things along. Unless…

Unless she had other ideas.

Something dark floated in the periphery of his mind.

"It's just with all that's happened…I won't deny we've had some good times together."

"Yes, we have." Times he'd hoped would get even better. Except Cassie was using the past tense. Was she simply being cautious about jumping into another relationship? If so, he couldn't blame her. "Are you worried because of how things ended with Darrin?"

"Yes. No." She hesitated before continuing. "I don't know where you saw this…" she motioned between the two of them "…going, but I need you to tell me. I want to make sure we're on the same page."

The "page" he'd been reading seconds earlier suddenly went blank. Because he was pretty sure that what was written on hers was something totally different from what was printed on his.

Okay, if she wanted to take things slower, he would do his damnedest to give her what she wanted. "I was hoping to continue like we have been. To take things one day at a time—see how it all plays out. No pressure—*none*—on either side."

There, he'd even cadenced the words, making sure they didn't come across as rushed. Or desperate.

Instead of smiling in relief, Cassie's fingers clenched around the keys, her face turning ashen.

"I'm not here to pressure you."

"I didn't say you were." He had no idea what was happening. Only that things were imploding in front of him, and he had no idea how to stop them. "I'm trying to take responsibility for my actions the best way I know how."

The best way wasn't the right way, evidently, because her arms went around her waist and her eyes closed for a few seconds. At first he thought she was going to be sick, like she'd been in his office.

He took a step forward, only to be stopped in his tracks when she looked at him again.

She wasn't feeling sick. Instead, there was a quiet resolve in her gaze that ripped at something inside him.

"I don't hold you responsible, Rafe. For anything. My pregnancy was an accident. You don't have to stick around."

A beat went by. Then two.

"Are you saying you don't want me to?"

Cassie's chin wobbled, and then her teeth dug into her bottom lip, leaving a mark in the soft flesh. "You know, I think I *am* saying that. It might be best for everyone."

Everyone. Except him.

She was letting him off the hook. Helping him dodge a bullet. Allowing him to skate by without facing the consequences.

Dammit!

Rafe could spin her words a thousand different ways, but no matter how hard he tried it boiled down to the same thing. Her vision of the future did not include him.

This was the very reason he never opened himself up to relationships. Because there was one thing he had never learned how to deal with. Not with his parents' deaths. And not with his brother Santi's disappearance afterwards. And that was how to tell someone he loved goodbye.

Well, it was time he learned.

And so Rafe did the only thing he could under the

circumstances. Without a word, he took his hip off her car and backed up a step to let her open the door.

He didn't say anything as she got in and shut the door behind her. He didn't try to protest as she started the engine and shifted the transmission into Reverse.

And the hardest thing of all…he didn't try to stop her when she backed the car out of the space and then slowly drove away.

CHAPTER TEN

CASSIE MEASURED THE newest baby's head. Perfect. Juliana Sanchez was right within the normal range, even though her mom had moved from a Zika-affected part of Brazil four months ago. In the last couple of weeks there had been no more confirmed cases of the virus. Either it was on a downswing or cases were going to come in on a cyclical basis, depending on the time of year women got pregnant.

It was her first day back at work after taking a two-week break to recoup her strength and try to get over Rafe. She'd failed miserably on that count.

Instead, she'd gone through her days a blubbery, waterlogged mess. There'd been no way she could have faced her tiny patients. Runny mascara and red eyes gave reassurance to no one. Especially not worried parents.

How many stages of grief were there again?

Too many to count, and she'd experienced every single one of them. Multiple times.

Rafe hadn't called since that devastating scene in the parking lot. Then again, she hadn't really expected him to.

What had she hoped to gain by confronting him like

that? Had she really thought that by asking him where he saw things going, he would profess his undying love to her and take her on a Caribbean cruise?

Not exactly. What she *had* hoped for was something more than a 'continue as they were…take things one day at a time and see where they went' kind of plan. As she'd stood there, she'd realized it wasn't enough. She'd lived her childhood that way, taking life one day at a time—one temporary relationship at a time. Now that she was an adult, she had the ability to change course. While Rafe had scrambled around for an answer that would placate her, that's precisely what she'd decided to do.

Even though doing so had split her heart in two.

She couldn't bear to see him day after day, knowing she loved him. Not when he'd handed her nothing to hold onto. It would destroy her. So she'd offered to cut him loose. And what had he done? He'd taken his newfound freedom and stepped away from her car, letting her drive away. He hadn't contacted her since. Didn't that tell her all she needed to know?

She forced a smile as she handed Juliana back to her mother. "Your baby is perfect."

So were hers. So far her twins were doing well. As was Cassie.

At least physically.

It was stupid. Rafe—like Darrin—was probably grateful he didn't have to pretend to feel something he didn't. She couldn't blame him. Right now she was a hormonal, neurotic wreck. Maybe he was counting his lucky stars that they hadn't gone further than they had.

But what about his babies? By doing what she had, she'd cut him out of their lives as well. At the time she'd told herself it was for their own good. Now she wasn't so sure.

She finished her visit with this patient and headed on to the next. She rounded the corner and was shocked to spot Carmelita wandering along the hallway, looking around as if she was lost.

Oh, great. The last thing she wanted to see was someone involved with the Valentino brothers. She could turn around and walk the other way, but Carmelita had already seen her, because her gaze cleared and she walked quickly toward her with a little wave that asked her to wait. "Cassandra!"

Closing her eyes, she tried to muster the strength needed to smile and make small talk. Then a thought hit her. Were the brothers okay?

Rafe…was he okay? Could something have happened?

She moved toward the woman, waiting through the customary kiss on the cheek before posing her question. "Is everything all right? Rafe?"

Carmelita shook her head, clenched fist over her heart. "I'm afraid not. Rafe is…"

She'd been right. He was hurt. Or worse. "Where is he?"

"In the air."

"Is he being medevaced in?" Panic swept through her. Why else would Carmelita be at the hospital? Had he been in an accident?

"Medevaced? I do not know this word."

"Is he being flown to the hospital?"

Her hand dropped back to her side. "No, but he should be. He will not listen to reason."

Cassie had no idea what the woman was talking about. "Does he need to see a doctor?"

The bodega manager smiled. "Yes, he does." She paused. "He needs...what do you call it? A head doctor. He is not seeing straight."

Her mind raced. Vision problems could indicate something serious. "You need to talk him into coming in, Carmelita. I can recommend a neurologist." She pulled out her smartphone and started to flip through the lists of phone numbers.

A touch to her hand stopped her. "Rafael does not need to see just any doctor. He needs to see you."

"I'm a neonatologist. A baby doctor." She thought for a second. "What about Dante? He's a neurologist. Can't he talk some sense into him?"

Carmelita's brown eyes looked into hers, a wealth of meaning in them. "No. He cannot. Santi and Alejandro have already tried talking. He will not listen."

Her heart stuttered. "I don't understand."

"Rafe has told you about his parents, no?"

"A little. And you mentioned that they'd been killed at the bodega."

"Mmm. Yes. But you did not know that his father lived for a short time afterward? It was hard for everyone. And Alejandro...a bullet hit him too. We almost lost him."

Cassie hadn't known that. But she'd seen Alejandro. He'd survived. "I'm glad he's okay. But I'm not sure what this has to do with me."

"No? Alejandro carries his father's heart."

Shock wheeled through her. She had to assume the woman didn't mean he literally carried his father's heart around in a box, so that must mean...

Before she could ask, Carmelita nodded. "Yes. It is true. Rafe…well, he wasn't ready to say goodbye to his *papi*. None of us were." She clasped her hands in front of her. "It is very difficult for him, even today. The thought of losing those he cares about. So he pushes people away. Then he does not have to make hard choices."

She tried to sift through the woman's words—to force her sluggish brain to function. In the end, though, it didn't really change things between her and Rafe. Or did it? "I'm so sorry, but I'm not sure why you're telling me all of this."

"That is something you must figure out for yourself." She leaned in and gave Cassie another kiss on the cheek. "But do not take too long."

Then she was gone, leaving Cassie standing there with her mouth open.

Had the bodega manager come to the hospital just to deliver that cryptic message?

He pushes people away. So he does not have to make hard choices.

Was that why he he'd talked about not putting pressure on anyone? She thought about the note and money he'd left before she'd woken up that first night. He hadn't wanted to face her. Had made sure neither of them had the other's contact information—not that she would have given it to him.

He hadn't wanted to take any chances that he could come to care for her or any other woman. Was that it?

And she'd made it easy for him. He hadn't needed to push her away. No. She'd pushed him away instead. For the very same reason. So she didn't have to make the hard choice of trusting him with her heart.

She reached back and tightened her ponytail. Damn. She could stand here speculating about this all day and come up with nothing. If Rafe couldn't be a big boy and face up to his fears, then did she really want him?

Her fingers went back to her hair—to the hair tie, actually. Although he claimed that first elastic band had gotten mixed up with his things accidentally, he'd kept it. And she'd found it. He'd never expected to see her again, and yet he hadn't tossed it into the garbage. He'd held onto it.

Why?

Because he couldn't toss aside that encounter as easily as he wanted to? They'd come together two more times.

She hadn't been able to resist him.

Was it the same for him?

If so, what was she supposed to do about it?

You must figure it out for yourself. But do not take too long.

Why? What was going to happen? Rafe would just move on to the next woman?

He could have done that at any time over the last couple of months. But he hadn't. Maybe that was what he'd wanted to talk to her about in the parking garage, only to have her cut him off.

So why was she standing here, doing nothing, instead of going over to his office and talking about this head on, rather than skating around the issue like she'd done the last time?

Fine. If that's what Carmelita meant, maybe that's what she would do.

Then, if the man really wanted to tell her goodbye, he was going to have to do it to her face.

* * *

She didn't get that face time. A half hour later, she walked out of his office building with a frown. He wasn't there.

So where was he? His condo? One of the receptionists had told her Rafe had taken the day off. She'd been nice enough to try calling him for her, but he hadn't picked up, and Cassie was loath to let the other woman leave him a message.

He's in the air.

Carmelita's strange words suddenly made sense. Of course he wasn't being medevaced to the hospital. He had taken that backpack-looking thing and gone flying. But where?

Wasn't there a beach at the northern end of Miami where there were always paragliders? She wasn't sure but she knew someone who would know. Someone who had told her that Rafe had been spending a lot of time in the air recently.

Dante. And because of the neurologist's meeting with Renato, she just so happened to have the man's number programmed into her cell phone...

CHAPTER ELEVEN

RAFE'S BOOTS TOUCHED down on a sparsely populated section of the beach, and he ran several feet to keep his balance while his paraglider continued to descend. When it finally drifted to the ground he shut his eyes, jaws clenched tight against the tide of emotion that rushed in.

Hell, instead of making him feel better, the two-hour flight had made him feel worse.

She doesn't want a relationship with you, Rafe. It's as obvious as the red on your paraglider.

She'd seemed softer after they'd had sex in the exam room. And then something had shifted in the two-day break afterward. Instead of talking it out and asking why, he had let her get in that car and drive out of his life.

And he couldn't get the damn image of her pale features out of his head. There had been something off about her behavior that day. But unless he wanted to confront her and demand to know what it was, he was stuck.

Or was he?

He unhooked himself from the harness and quickly stretched out his paraglider wing until it lay flat. Then, folding the material back on itself until it was a manageable size, he took the stuff sack from his back. Then he loaded the craft into it and wound the cord until everything was stowed away. In the process, he came to a decision.

He wasn't going to fly away from his problems any more. Because they were always waiting for him when he came back down. If things were over with Cassie, then they were going to be really over. And that meant getting closure. The closure he'd never gotten when his parents had died.

He would head over to Cassie's apartment and ask some direct questions. And then, if he was right, and she no longer wanted to see him, he would be done.

Shouldering the pack, he turned to walk down the beach, only to be stopped in his tracks. Because there stood the person he'd just been agonizing over. The person he'd come here to forget.

He dragged a hand through his hair, not quite trusting his eyes. When he looked closer, though, she was still there.

Cassie.

Wearing beige shorts and a white shirt, she held a wide-brimmed hat on her head with one hand. And in the other she held...

Hair ties?

He stared at the clear package, the crush of memories threatening to drive him into the sand. Had she come here to rub salt into his wounds?

"I didn't expect to see you here." And if that wasn't the stupidest thing to say, he didn't know what was.

"I know. But Carmelita came to the hospital, and I had to come."

Her hair blew freely around her shoulders for once, the blond locks making his fingers itch to touch them. To stroke them. None of which he could do.

For several seconds he just stood there without saying anything.

She saved him the trouble. "Mind if we sit awhile?"

Not waiting for an answer, she dropped onto the sand with a light, graceful movement, setting the hair-tie package on the ground and patting the spot next to her.

His eyes pored over her figure, trying to memorize everything about her. Her stomach still showed no signs of her pregnancy, and her... Wait. Carmelita had gone to the hospital? Why? His heart stopped for a second before it started beating again.

"Is everything okay?"

"No, but I hope it will be soon." She nodded at the package. "I brought you a present."

He carefully lowered himself onto the beach, leaving plenty of distance between them, just in case. "Present?"

She straightened. "I lost enough of these that I had to buy a new package. Then I thought, if you liked them that much I would save you the trouble of stealing any more of them."

And how exactly would he do that? She'd said she didn't want to see him again.

Except she was here. Bearing gifts.

Had he misunderstood her? He tried to recall her exact words, only to lose them in the chaotic mix of emotions he'd felt that day. He set his stuff sack down, elbows going to his knees as he glanced over at her and then out to sea, where other paragliders were still hanging suspended in the air. "You look good."

"So do you. I've never gotten to see you fly. Do you really like it?"

His throat tightened. He had at one time but recently it had lost some of its appeal. "I did. I do." He tried to clear his thoughts. "Why exactly did Carmelita come to see you?"

Her finger traced a pattern in the sand.

"She said you push people away. I came to ask you if that's true."

He gave a rough snort. "Carmelita should mind her own damn business. What did she say anyway?"

"She said you'd had a hard time after your dad died. That you still do." Her hand stopped drawing.

"That is pretty much the understatement of the year."

"I can't imagine how difficult it had to be." She paused. "How have your brothers dealt with it?"

He turned his head and looked at her, his gaze suddenly going blurry.

Hell, no. Not now.

"Dealt with what? The fact that I signed the order to disconnect our father's life support—to have his chest cracked open and his heart removed? Maybe you should ask them."

Cassie's mouth dropped open and then snapped shut. Her hand covered his. "You? I had no idea. I am so sorry."

"I thought you said Carmelita told you."

"No. She told me about the transplant. And that you push people away because of your father's death."

Okay, so the bodega manager hadn't spilled all the details. He'd done it for her.

Time to get to the point, though, before something inside him broke.

"Why are you here, Cassie?"

"I'm here because Carmelita made me realize something. You're not the only one who pushes people away. I do too." Her fingers threaded through his. "And I don't want to do that anymore."

His thoughts shifted so suddenly he thought he might have whiplash. "You don't?"

"No."

He tightened his grip on her hand. "That is… Hell, you might not believe this, but I was going to drive over to your house today for that very same reason."

"You were?"

"I've been trying to figure out what drove that whole conversation in the parking lot that day, but I keep coming up blank. You said you push people away. Why?"

"Because I don't trust them to stay."

"I don't understand." Actually, he understood all too well. He didn't trust people to stay either.

She shifted her body until she was looking right at him. "I'm going to lay it on the line here, Rafe. And if you knew my background you would know how hard this is for me…"

He leaned closer, something in the quiet urgency of her words pulling at him. "It's okay. Tell me."

"You have such a strong bond with your brothers— your parents. I'm envious, because I didn't have that. I grew up without a home." She bit her lip for a second. "That's not exactly true. I had homes…a long line of them, actually. I just never knew how long each would last. Or when a car might pull into the driveway to take me to the next drop-off point."

"But your mom and dad—"

"Are wonderful, and I love them dearly. But they didn't come into my life until I was a teenager. They adopted me. Until that time I was in the foster-care system."

He sucked in a quick breath. Maybe he wasn't the only one who kept secrets. "I didn't know."

"It's not something I shout from the rooftops. Only a few people—like Bonnie—know. Anyway, it makes me cautious about relationships." She shrugged. "When I realized I cared about you, I was terrified that you didn't feel the same way. That, like all those foster homes, you would disappear from my life...from my babies' lives. I don't want that for them."

"You think I would do that?"

"I thought you might. You talked about not putting pressure on either of us, about taking things one day at a time—as if you could simply walk away if things didn't go the way you wanted them to." One hand moved to her stomach. "But after Carmelita's visit I decided I needed to be sure. So if you don't want to be with me for the next fifty or so years, I need you to tell me in no uncertain terms. So I can move on. So *we* can move on."

It was as if he were paralyzed. Hope was swirling all around him, and yet he couldn't move. Couldn't speak.

Fifty or so years? He was half-afraid he was imagining this whole thing. Could you get altitude sickness from paragliding?

Cassie watched him for a few more seconds, then she grabbed the hair ties and climbed to her feet, her hat blowing from her head and tumbling down the beach. She ignored it. "Okay. I guess I have my answer."

He was off the ground in an instant. "No. You don't. I…"

Moving to stand in front of her, he cupped her face, searching for the words that would make her believe him. "I'm not good at this. And I don't know how to do relationships." His thumbs stroked across her cheeks. "You're right. My brothers and I have a strong bond. Because they're blood. But choosing to open myself up to someone else, to believe they'll always be there… It's hard."

"It's hard for me too, Rafe. I'm just as afraid as you are. But we can't keep pushing away these chances at happiness."

"I know." He rested his chin on her head, the sweet scent of her hair filling him. "I swore I would never be in a position like I was with my father. To have to say goodbye to someone I loved. So I avoided getting involved. With anyone."

"Is that why you left the hotel without waking me up?"

"Yes. Because even that night I knew something was different, that something dangerous could happen if I stayed. It happened anyway. I love you, Cassie."

There, he'd said the words that had been bubbling in his head for the last two weeks.

She leaned back and took his hands, the hair-tie package held between them. "I love you too. And it was killing me to think you might never feel the same way."

"You have no idea how hard it was to let you drive away that day."

"I think I might. What happened to your parents and Alejandro was beyond terrible. But that doesn't mean that every relationship you have will end in tragedy." Her grip tightened. "You felt alone back then. I get it. But you weren't. Not really. Your brothers were there. And if you let me, I'll be there too. You don't have to do life alone."

His throat worked, a rush of emotions clogging his chest, cutting off his breath. Then he dragged her close, holding her tight. "I was afraid I was going to lose you too. When you said it was better if I didn't hang around—"

"I lied." Her words were muffled by his chest. "It's not better. I love you, Rafe—more than I imagined possible. Let us in. Please."

"You were already there that first night. I thought if I just slipped away before you woke up, I could get rid of that feeling. I was wrong." He bent to kiss her.

"So, what are we going to do?"

"We're going to stop pushing each other away, for starters. I think we can let this little package be our guide." He let go of her and held up the hair ties. "I want to take the elastic out of your hair. Every night— like I did those times we were together—and I'm going put it into a jar. Each day will be a new hair tie…a new beginning. When that jar is full, we'll start another one."

"And if I chop my hair off, and we no longer need the ties?"

"Then our daughters will use them."

"How do you know they're going to be girls?"

Rafe smiled, the joy in his heart growing with every word she said. She was talking like there actually was a forever. He held onto that, letting it steep in his soul. "I don't. But there's always the next baby."

"The next? Exactly how many children do you want?" The alarm in her voice was overridden by her laughter. "Scratch that. I'm sure my parents would be extremely happy if we had several."

"Marry me? So we can get started on those fifty years."

"Fifty years. That sounds heavenly."

"So is that a yes?" He didn't quite trust that this was actually happening. He wanted…no, he *needed* to know she was all in. Just like he was.

She laid her cheek against his, her voice whispering in his ear. "It's a yes. Yes to marriage. Yes to life with you."

"I know you didn't want to rush into a relationship, but this is as slow as I can go."

She bit his earlobe, sending sweet heat flooding through his system. "I happen to know you can go pretty darn slow."

"I can't think when you do that." He tried again, some tiny part of him still needing reassurance. "I want the wedding to be soon."

"It can be tomorrow, if you want. As long as we're together." Then she stepped back, her teeth nibbling at her lower lip. "Oh, wait. There might be a problem with that."

He frowned, wondering if he'd gotten his hopes up for nothing. "What kind of problem?"

"A Bonnie kind of problem." She took the package of hair ties from him and tossed it onto the sand.

"Bonnie, as in your friend?"

"Yep." She rubbed the edge of his chin with her

thumb. Rafe understood immediately why his cat loved that so much.

Damn. He tried to find the thread of their conversation again. "Bonnie is a problem?"

Her thumb worked its way down his neck with soft, hypnotic strokes. "She said if we ever got together she would have to do something at our wedding. And if it's tomorrow…"

Hell, the woman could walk across hot coals, as long as it ended with Cassie becoming his wife. "Anything she wants."

"Anything?"

"That's what I said."

"You might be sorry when you hear what it is. She wants to sing a song and dedicate it to us."

His body was already thrumming under her touch, and soon he wouldn't care what Bonnie did or didn't want to do. The sooner they got back to his condo the better. "Still not seeing the problem."

Cassie laughed and moved in close, her body crowding his with purposeful intent that he was hoping to accommodate very, very soon.

"You will," she said, going up on tiptoe and brushing her lips across his. "Because as much as she might like to think otherwise, Bonnie can't sing."

EPILOGUE

THEY HAD SURVIVED Bonnie's singing. All of them. And the four months since their wedding had been filled with love and laughter. And blessed stability. For her. And the babies growing in her belly.

Cassie stood on the beach this warm November afternoon, watching her husband soar high overhead, the red of his paraglider easily visible against the pale sky. She'd always been afraid of flying, of hanging in space with nothing beneath her feet, but as the soft grains of sand filtered between her toes she realized she had already reached new heights. And she was no longer afraid.

Rafe had become her haven. A safe place to land. And she was grateful their children would be able to have a secure home like the one her adoptive parents had provided for her.

They were surrounded by love. By Rafe's brothers and their wives, by Carmelita. And by her mom and dad. And most of all, they had each other.

Rafe waved to her as he went by, his craft much lower on this pass. She couldn't believe she'd agreed to go up with him after the babies were born. But as long as he was with her, she could do anything. Even paraglide.

His feet touched the ground fifty yards in front of her, and Cassie was off, jogging the best she could toward him, cradling her belly in her hands. And then she was in his arms even before he'd gotten out of his harness.

"You looked good up there," she murmured, kissing the edge of his chin.

"You looked pretty good down here. I couldn't wait to be back on the ground."

He let her go long enough to release the straps and fold up his equipment, then he slung it over his shoulder. "You shouldn't be running any more."

"It's fine. I'm not even seven months along. Besides, I'm a doctor, remember?" Wrapping her arm around his waist, she couldn't resist giving that taut backside a quick squeeze. "I know something else that's fine."

"Cassie…"

He'd been worried about everything recently, scolding her for this or that. She knew it came from those old fears of losing those closest to him, but that wasn't going to happen. Cassie had no intention of going anywhere. She would fight with all of her being to stay with him.

"Dr. Davi said there's no reason we can't." She gave him another squeeze. "Besides, you're supposed to indulge your pregnant wife's cravings."

"Food cravings."

"Any craving." She laughed. "If I remember correctly, we've been known to combine the two. Maybe I should taste test you this time around."

He groaned, stopping to drop a kiss on her mouth

that was anything but chaste. "Enough. I give up. Let's get you home."

Cassie wove her fingers through his and they started down the beach, her body already humming a familiar tune.

As impatient as she was to be with him, she was in no real hurry. They had time.

Fifty-some-odd years, if she remembered right. And she intended to use each and every second of them to make Rafe as happy as he made her.

Today and always.

* * * * *

Look out for the final instalment of the
HOT LATIN DOCS *quartet*
DANTE'S SHOCK PROPOSAL
by Amalie Berlin

And if you missed where it all started check out
SANTIAGO'S CONVENIENT FIANCÉE
by Annie O'Neil
ALEJANDRO'S SEXY SECRET
by Amy Ruttan

Available now!

MILLS & BOON®
Hardback – February 2017

ROMANCE

The Last Di Sione Claims His Prize	Maisey Yates
Bought to Wear the Billionaire's Ring	Cathy Williams
The Desert King's Blackmailed Bride	Lynne Graham
Bride by Royal Decree	Caitlin Crews
The Consequence of His Vengeance	Jennie Lucas
The Sheikh's Secret Son	Maggie Cox
Acquired by Her Greek Boss	Chantelle Shaw
Vows They Can't Escape	Heidi Rice
The Sheikh's Convenient Princess	Liz Fielding
The Unforgettable Spanish Tycoon	Christy McKellen
The Billionaire of Coral Bay	Nikki Logan
Her First-Date Honeymoon	Katrina Cudmore
Their Meant-to-Be Baby	Caroline Anderson
A Mummy for His Baby	Molly Evans
Rafael's One Night Bombshell	Tina Beckett
A Forever Family for the Army Doc	Meredith Webber
The Nurse and the Single Dad	Dianne Drake
The Heir's Unexpected Baby	Jules Bennett
From Enemies to Expecting	Kat Cantrell

MILLS & BOON®
Large Print – February 2017

ROMANCE

The Return of the Di Sione Wife	Caitlin Crews
Baby of His Revenge	Jennie Lucas
The Spaniard's Pregnant Bride	Maisey Yates
A Cinderella for the Greek	Julia James
Married for the Tycoon's Empire	Abby Green
Indebted to Moreno	Kate Walker
A Deal with Alejandro	Maya Blake
A Mistletoe Kiss with the Boss	Susan Meier
A Countess for Christmas	Christy McKellen
Her Festive Baby Bombshell	Jennifer Faye
The Unexpected Holiday Gift	Sophie Pembroke

HISTORICAL

Awakening the Shy Miss	Bronwyn Scott
Governess to the Sheikh	Laura Martin
An Uncommon Duke	Laurie Benson
Mistaken for a Lady	Carol Townend
Kidnapped by the Highland Rogue	Terri Brisbin

MEDICAL

Seduced by the Sheikh Surgeon	Carol Marinelli
Challenging the Doctor Sheikh	Amalie Berlin
The Doctor She Always Dreamed Of	Wendy S. Marcus
The Nurse's Newborn Gift	Wendy S. Marcus
Tempting Nashville's Celebrity Doc	Amy Ruttan
Dr White's Baby Wish	Sue MacKay

MILLS & BOON®
Hardback – March 2017

ROMANCE

Secrets of a Billionaire's Mistress	Sharon Kendrick
Claimed for the De Carrillo Twins	Abby Green
The Innocent's Secret Baby	Carol Marinelli
The Temporary Mrs Marchetti	Melanie Milburne
A Debt Paid in the Marriage Bed	Jennifer Hayward
The Sicilian's Defiant Virgin	Susan Stephens
Pursued by the Desert Prince	Dani Collins
The Forgotten Gallo Bride	Natalie Anderson
Return of Her Italian Duke	Rebecca Winters
The Millionaire's Royal Rescue	Jennifer Faye
Proposal for the Wedding Planner	Sophie Pembroke
A Bride for the Brooding Boss	Bella Bucannon
Their Secret Royal Baby	Carol Marinelli
Her Hot Highland Doc	Annie O'Neil
His Pregnant Royal Bride	Amy Ruttan
Baby Surprise for the Doctor Prince	Robin Gianna
Resisting Her Army Doc Rival	Susan MacKay
A Month to Marry the Midwife	Fiona McArthur
Billionaire's Baby Promise	Sarah M. Anderson
Seduce Me, Cowboy	Maisey Yates

MILLS & BOON®
Large Print – March 2017

ROMANCE

Di Sione's Virgin Mistress	Sharon Kendrick
Snowbound with His Innocent Temptation	Cathy Williams
The Italian's Christmas Child	Lynne Graham
A Diamond for Del Rio's Housekeeper	Susan Stephens
Claiming His Christmas Consequence	Michelle Smart
One Night with Gael	Maya Blake
Married for the Italian's Heir	Rachael Thomas
Christmas Baby for the Princess	Barbara Wallace
Greek Tycoon's Mistletoe Proposal	Kandy Shepherd
The Billionaire's Prize	Rebecca Winters
The Earl's Snow-Kissed Proposal	Nina Milne

HISTORICAL

The Runaway Governess	Liz Tyner
The Winterley Scandal	Elizabeth Beacon
The Queen's Christmas Summons	Amanda McCabe
The Discerning Gentleman's Guide	Virginia Heath

MEDICAL

A Daddy for Her Daughter	Tina Beckett
Reunited with His Runaway Bride	Robin Gianna
Rescued by Dr Rafe	Annie Claydon
Saved by the Single Dad	Annie Claydon
Sizzling Nights with Dr Off-Limits	Janice Lynn
Seven Nights with Her Ex	Louisa Heaton

MILLS & BOON®

Why shop at millsandboon.co.uk?

Each year, thousands of romance readers find their perfect read at millsandboon.co.uk. That's because we're passionate about bringing you the very best romantic fiction. Here are some of the advantages of shopping at www.millsandboon.co.uk:

* **Get new books first**—you'll be able to buy your favourite books one month before they hit the shops

* **Get exclusive discounts**—you'll also be able to buy our specially created monthly collections, with up to 50% off the RRP

* **Find your favourite authors**—latest news, interviews and new releases for all your favourite authors and series on our website, plus ideas for what to try next

* **Join in**—once you've bought your favourite books, don't forget to register with us to rate, review and join in the discussions

Visit **www.millsandboon.co.uk**
for all this and more today!